MARK CAREW was born in Wales and brought up near Sudbury, Suffolk. He studied Biochemistry at King's College, London, and received a PhD in Cell Physiology from Cambridge in 1995. After post docs in Cambridge and North Carolina, he worked as a medical writer before joining Kingston University where he was an Associate Professor until 2019. His stories have appeared in print and online in literary magazines. His debut, *The Book of Alexander* was published by Salt in 2018 and was nominated for Kingston University's Big Read Project.

ALSO BY MARK CAREW

The Book of Alexander (2018)

MARK CAREW
MAGNUS

SALT

CROMER

PUBLISHED BY SALT PUBLISHING 2019

2 4 6 8 10 9 7 5 3 1

First published in Great Britain in 2019 by
Salt Publishing Ltd
12 Norwich Road, Cromer, Norfolk NR27 0AX United Kingdom

www.saltpublishing.com

Salt Publishing Limited Reg. No. 5293401

A CIP catalogue record for this book is available from the British Library

ISBN 978 1 78463 204 5 (Paperback edition)
ISBN 978 1 78463 205 2 (Electronic edition)

Typeset in Neacademia by Salt Publishing

Printed and bound in Great Britain by Clays Ltd, Elcograf S.p.A

To all the heroes – never give up.

CHAPTER 1

Now we shall hear the might of kings, and about time.

No more Mister Nice Guy, no more bleeding-heart liberal. Professor: sort this unruly individual out!

'Magnus! For the last time. You are not to go up there!' Professor Erik Nordveit was standing at the base of the weather tower, dressed in a green anorak and looking most unhappy. 'Please come down.'

Please? Would Alfred or Bø, his illustrious ancestors, have asked so nicely? Magnus was disappointed. Where was the shotgun, or the whip, when they were needed? Didn't the Professor know that his student had messed with the best of the country's counsellors and still no-one had any idea of how he really ticked? The spinning cups of the anemometer at the top of the weather tower could wait. It was the first day of the field trip, and there was plenty of time for mayhem later in the week. Magnus began to descend the tower. Now he hung only a few metres above the Professor, a man whose patience and mental strength he would test to the limit. He formed a gobbet of phlegm in his mouth and considered dropping it on to the Professor's head.

'Come on,' said Erik, 'all the way down, please.'

He treats me like a child. Doesn't he know that I am Magnus the Great?

The weather monitoring tower outside the cabin had

fascinated him as soon as their party had landed on the island. The tower was ten metres tall, made of aluminium, and stabilised by six steel hawsers set into concrete blocks in the ground. There were various instruments sited on the way up, and at the top of the tower was the anemometer: a horizontal metal bar with four spinning silver cups on a short pole at one end. The device was attached to electronics which measured wind-speed. At the other end of the bar was a short vertical sprue with a black fin, which turned into the wind and gave its direction. Magnus dearly wanted to fondle those delicate revolving cups, and to stroke the tail fin, but the Professor was watching him.

The Professor's attention was then diverted from Magnus to a dark green moss that had taken his eye by his feet. He bent down to investigate. Magnus was disgusted. Here was a grown man, a man of power, who with one stroke of his pen could make or break a student's university career. But instead of driving a Lamborghini, or wearing the latest designer fashion, this man got excited about mosses: the most primitive plants on the planet.

Magnus formulated his plan. He prepared for the perfect moment to launch his glistening missile towards the Professor's pate. Such a direct attack would have to be done with skill. A hit would have to be blamed on one of the seabirds, the gulls and petrels circling overhead. As an alibi, he spat first into his own hand and rubbed the spittle on the side of his face. He waited for another gob of saliva to form in his mouth. When it was ready, he adjusted for wind speed and direction. The disgusting dollop squeezed out from between his lips and landed on the green baize carpet of mosses by the Professor's feet.

The alpha, the pack leader, the daddy, the big brain didn't even move, but carried on with his botanical inspection. Mosses were a living detector of metal pollution in the air, a bio-indicator species, the field trip synopsis had explained, and Professor Nordveit was fascinated by the subject.

Magnus jumped down from the tower and landed with a thud on the ground. He scuffed up some of the mosses and kicked the stupid green and brown clumps towards where the Professor knelt.

Erik didn't notice a thing and when he stood up, Magnus was towering over him. Erik stepped back. 'What did you see from up there, Magnus? Was it something that you could not see from down here?'

'Yes, Professor. I saw my future.'

Erik was intrigued. 'What do you mean?'

Magnus the Great smiled inside but his mouth was set firm. In his future the island of Svindel was his alone and no others were allowed to set foot on it. 'I saw myself as a giant eagle, flying high above the world, with nothing to worry about.'

'Good!' said Erik. 'I'm really pleased to hear it.'

The Professor beamed at him and Magnus could not bear to look at his happy face. Why are clever people so stupid, he thought? Why do they always think the best of other people?

Magnus walked away until he stood on top of one of the many boulders scattered on the green carpet. The island was quite small and could easily be managed by one person. There was the cabin with its golden roof shining under the midnight sun. There was the white university motor boat bobbing gently at the jetty. A network of earthen paths ran east-west through the green carpet of precious mosses from jetty to boulder field, then on to the copse of trees above the fishing rocks. The eastern shore looked over other islands and back to the mainland. Just visible on a clear day were the fjords around the coast of Tromsø where they had departed from their alma mater.

Now when he looked out over the island it was as if Magnus had suddenly become Erik's son. The thought hit him with quite a shock. Why had Erik handed the island down to him, and not to his wife or daughter? Magnus had not known his own father, so perhaps that had been the reason why? Or perhaps Erik recognised in Magnus the necessary qualities few people would have to manage a small island on their own? A tiny island, two kilometres off the coast of Norway, uninhabited because it was beyond the reach of telecommunications with the mainland. How many people would truly enjoy living there alone? It would be wonderful if you liked rocks, boulders, mosses and other lowly plants, because save for a few fir trees near the fishing shore, that was it for scenery. No other plants had the energy to move up the exposed mountainside and grow any taller. If it wasn't for the folly of man, in the form of pollution and climate change, no-one would have been at all interested in the place.

But what Magnus was really interested in was at the northern end of the island. At seven hundred and fifty metres' elevation, according to the map in the cabin, was a mountain called Trollveggen. What lay behind Trollveggen on its hidden, seaward side? Did the Professor think that Magnus was the man for exploring the place and reporting back? Had he been impressed so far with how his most interesting student had handled himself?

What about that moment of bravado from Magnus, when

4

they had arrived from the west and landed at the jetty, the Professor at the helm. The sea had been choppy and of course Linnéa, the most annoying of the students, was terrified. Mette had sat next to her, trying to keep her calm. The two young women had been briefed on how their boat and their personal floatation devices were state of the art, but it hadn't sunk in. So it was left to Magnus to stand up at the front of the boat, gulping in the sea breeze, arms outstretched as if he were the mast and sails, and shield them from the worst of the wind.

There was the noise of an immense flapping, as if a monstrous bird flew overhead. Magnus took a moment to dismiss such an idea and soon recognised the source of the distraction: the blue tarpaulin covering the boat was lifting off aft of the wheelhouse. The heavy canvas material had been tied up with rope through ringlets and guys, but somehow it had come undone at one edge and was blowing up in the wind.

Magnus watched the Professor jog down to the jetty. Erik would be questioning his own knots, which had been double-checked by Per, who was an experienced fisherman, and by Jonas, who thought he knew everything. The fools had trusted Magnus to be last off the boat, but perhaps Per wasn't so foolish. He had caught Magnus with a look that said he knew his type. But no one would see the true colours of Magnus the Great until they had been revealed, and by then it would be too late.

The sea lapped at the shore and shoved at the boat, distracting the Professor and making his job more difficult. Magnus saw his chance, put one boot on the tower, climbed up to the instrument panel, and placed his hands inside. He groped and fumbled until he grabbed the leads going into the barometric pressure sensor. Then he pulled. The weather for that day was remarkably changeable. He stood up and blew into the air temperature sensor, a long white tube with a bulbous end, which was set two metres off the ground and level with his shoulders. For a few seconds, the ambient air temperature registered a huge increase. He found the solar radiance sensor and smeared the glass dome with soil he picked up from the ground. Today became a surprisingly dark day. Then he climbed up the tower so quickly that he felt the structure sway with his weight. At the top he took a great lungful of the lovely breeze and let the wind blow out his cheeks. Gulp in the breeze, eat it like raw fish, raw everything. His lips pulled back into a beak, and he blew at the spinning silver cups. Look out, world; a hurricane is coming!

There was laughter from the cabin. The other students on the trip were playing cards. Linnéa, Mette, Per and Jonas would be sitting around the table enjoying a game without him. Their jollity reached him through windows that were pushed open a crack for ventilation. Laugh while you can, Magnus thought.

Erik returned from the jetty. The blue tarpaulin was now even more securely fastened over the stern and midsection of the bright white boat. Magnus watched him make a point of stepping over and around the green mossy islands, as if it was bad luck to touch any of the ridiculous plants. He even used a hand-crank torch, which he wound up periodically, to show his path. The light in the sky had dimmed a little, it was true, although in June at this latitude the sun never disappeared entirely. Thor's arse, exclaimed Magnus inwardly; he hated the way the Professor modelled acceptable behaviour.

Erik reached the tower and sighed when he saw Magnus

above him. 'Up there again? You look like King Kong!' He placed his hands on his hips and laughed a little.

Very good, Professor, at least show a bit of spirit in battle.

The door to the cabin opened and Linnéa, the stuck-up trust fund girl, anxious for every mark she could induce by deploying her sweet smile, asked the Professor if he would like to play cards. Erik agreed. 'Come on, Magnus, time to go inside.'

Magnus considered his options. It wasn't time to be completely unruly yet. He was tired, and he needed a good night's sleep. His broken boots clanged out a diminishing scale on the metal tower as he descended. The pain on the right side under his ribs came back. He knew his eyes would be bad already.

'Thank you, Magnus. I'm glad you are taking such an interest in climatology, but the tower is not designed to be climbed upon. It actually hinges at the bottom and can be lowered for maintenance.' Erik pointed at his feet. 'Your boots need mending. The soles are coming away from the uppers.'

Magnus just shrugged. He stood outside the cabin door and waited for the Professor to enter first. No doubt his superior would think that Magnus was showing the appropriate deference and good manners.

The cabin door was oak and set in a frame that shone gold like the roof. Emblazoned in the centre of the door was the university crest: two seabirds passing parallel to one another. Erik pushed open the door and stepped inside the porch to remove his boots. Magnus contemplated the Professor's bald spot as it presented in front of him; it was at such an easy height to strike with the side of his hand. He wondered also about the strength of the back of the human skull, and of the force needed to dislodge the skull from the spine, and then the moment passed. He tucked his own enormous head down inside the doorway and went inside the cabin.

CHAPTER 2

E RIK TOOK OFF his shoes and put them neatly in the rack by the front door. He padded in his socks into the main room of the cabin. Linnéa was talking with Mette, a happy student found in the middle of the university's new café-style teaching rooms with her friends.

'Professor, is it true that your family owns the cabin and the island?' asked Linnéa.

'Yes, it is true. I am fourth in the line of the Nordveits. My grandfather, a man called Bø, claimed the island for Norway, and defended it from Swedish interest.'

'The cabin is wonderful,' said Mette. 'It's so well furnished.'

'Thank you. My wife and daughter are responsible, not me!'

The cabin was very spacious, with one long dining table surrounded by chairs in the middle of the central room. While the chairs were straight backed and local, the tablecloth was woven from a much more southerly country or continent, Spain or even Africa. Three curtained windows down each side of the cabin let in the ever-present midnight sun. The interior of the cabin glowed with a mixture of warm colours and was freshened with the greenery of many plants. One magnificent plant, with a tall flower stalk and thick fleshy leaves, dominated the middle of a hexagon-shaped side table. Each of the six windowsills had plants hung with red and white flowers. This was how Erik liked his cabin. A cupboard near the dormitory featured careful wooden fluting and was Nordic, a family heirloom.

Near the front door was the modern, well-equipped kitchen. At the far end of the cabin was the dormitory, and next to that the bathroom. Erik washed his hands in the basin, which, along with the toilet and shower, were supplied by a tank of rainwater collected from the golden roof. The lights on the four stone pillars in the main cabin flickered briefly. The diesel generator in the basement hummed a little louder. The two-bar gas heaters either side of the cabin were warming up, turning pink then red. This was his cabin and he loved it.

'Did your ancestor Bø use the island as an ecological outpost?' asked Jonas. He was a tall, slender young man, earnest in lectures, always in the front row with Linnéa.

'No, that's a very modern idea,' said Erik. 'Grandfather Bø lived in a cave on Trollveggen'. He indicated the mountain at the northern end of the island. 'Bø was the island's constant defender. Friends brought him in food and supplies. I don't think he ever left the place. How he managed to further our line, I don't know.'

'Must have been a nice warm cave,' said Per. 'Must have got someone interested.' He came out of the kitchen with a cup of tea. Per dipped in and out of lectures, but he did all the assessments and passed the exams. Linnéa followed him with a glass of drinking water, drawn from one of many blue forty-litre bottles stored in the basement.

'My father, Alfred,' said Erik, 'was credited with the building of a rudimentary wooden cabin on this spot.' He thumped the heel of his foot on the wooden floor. 'He also carried on Bø's paranoia. The island was continually manned during the last world war by a small handful of our men. Any enemy reconnaissance troops who arrived soon disappeared.'

Erik was holding court now, the students sitting around him. Even Magnus, standing behind him in the porch, listened intently.

'The island began to get noticed because of the repeated loss of the scouts who landed here. It even led once to a direct aerial attack by the enemy. The bombs destroyed the cabin, but of course Alfred and his men were hiding elsewhere. The enemy landed, but soon lost interest and moved on. Alfred restored the cabin as a refuge, and somehow tempted my mother to stay with him. I was one of four children born to them.' He showed them photographs of his ancestors on the stone walls, as he did every year to the students on the field trip.

Erik looked with pride around the well-furnished cabin. 'I was always fascinated by tales of this place, a cabin on a faraway island in the middle of nowhere. But when the land passed to me, I had no idea what to do with it. It is too remote for livestock, and the soil and climate are not suitable for agriculture. Then, one day, I was sitting in my office on campus. I read a paper about an environmental monitoring network that needed sites to look for atmospheric pollutants. And that's what put the island of Svindel on the map.' He smiled at them all.

Erik left the students and walked the length of the cabin, which was long enough to hold foot races. In the dormitory at the back he had a view, out of a small window, of the sea. The mainland was a suggestion in the distance. Accommodation was five bunk beds, enough to sleep ten people. Numbers were down on this trip, obviously, because they had Magnus along, but at least Linnéa, Mette, Per and Jonas each had a bottom bunk. Magnus had decided to take the top bunk above Erik, which Erik hadn't been that keen about, but rather him than anyone else.

Like the rest of the cabin, the dormitory was a homely place. His wife, Marta, and his daughter, Eva, had chosen the bedding. Marta had sourced thick blankets from the Sami people further north in Lapland. The bunk beds were made from a few pine trees native to the island. Eva had painted the room in restful shades of green, so that they all dreamed of mosses when they slept.

Erik changed out of his travelling clothes, still wet from sea spray from the boat ride in and put on jeans and a warm T-shirt. When he returned to the main room the pack of cards was still in the middle of the table, but no-one was playing.

Slumped by the main cabin door was Magnus, who seemed to be waiting for the group to acknowledge his existence. He had removed his boots, which were in a poor state, broken down, cracked and split. His socks were thin and his toes stuck out through ugly holes. He needed proper walking socks, not more designer-labelled gear that was not up to the job. Erik went over and asked Magnus to come and play cards, and would he like a cup of tea or spiced honey? Magnus just shrugged, so Erik left him to it. He noticed that a strange stale odour hung around Magnus, like that of cabbage stored too long in the open.

Instead of cards, Jonas started a round of storytelling with the other students. He placed a red baseball cap backwards on his head; a tuft of blonde hair stood up through the gap. Linnéa stood up and rearranged the cap to face forwards. All the students laughed at this modification, but Magnus remained po-faced.

Jonas brought the tips of his fingers together and thought for a moment. 'We start on an island at the tip of an archipelago in the Norwegian Sea. The island is close to a famous vortex of water where the fishing boats never go. At the end of the island there is a beach. Oh yes, and there is also a salt water swimming pool surrounded by trees.' Jonas leaned back on the sofa. 'Your go next,' he told Mette.

Mette, her face now partly hidden under the hood of a university sweatshirt, was sitting next to Linnéa. The two young women touched arms; Mette's milk chocolate contrasting with Linnéa's snow white.

'Every morning a young man came along to the swimming pool for his early morning swim,' Mette said.

The students waited for more, but Mette grimaced. She indicated that Linnéa should continue the story.

Linnéa bit her lip. 'Every morning the man had his swim and did many lengths of the pool. Then, one day, something different happened.' She nudged Per, who was sitting next to her eating a pain au chocolat.

Per scratched his head. He had little hair on his head, but the hint of a hairy chest rose up over the top of his grey T-shirt. He finished his mouthful. 'One day the man went for his normal morning swim and saw a pain au chocolat floating on the surface of the water.'

'Like it, Per,' said Jonas. 'Professor, it's your turn.'

Erik nursed a mug of hot spiced honey in his hands. 'The young man, whose name was Per, swam around the pain au chocolat he saw floating in the pool. He liked these French pastries very much. Finally, he took a bite.'

The story passed back to Jonas, who was thinking hard, but not getting anywhere.

Then Magnus spoke up from where he was sitting at the entrance of the cabin. 'Per was raised up into the air. There was a hook in the pastry and the hook cut into his mouth.'

'Ugh!' said Linnéa.

'No, that's good,' said Erik. 'Who can carry the story on?' But everyone was looking at the floor.

'I will carry it on,' said Magnus. He rose to his feet. His head bent against the roof of the cabin as if his neck was broken. 'There was a noisy flapping of giant wings. An enormous bluebird held the line in its mouth. The bird hauled the man called Per out of the pool and up into the branches of a fir tree.'

'Very inventive, Magnus, well done,' said Erik, not realising that the other students looked dismayed.

Magnus carried on. 'The enormous bluebird took the hook out of Per's mouth with its beak.' Magnus looked at Per throughout. 'Then the bluebird picked up Per and knocked his head against the tree branch until he was unconscious.'

Linnéa covered her ears. 'I don't want to hear any more.'

'How about a lovely ghost story?' asked Jonas. 'Or a whodunnit? I read a few English classics over Easter, they were really good.'

'We've got a good murder mystery, right here, although it's a little macabre,' Erik said. He seemed impressed with Magnus, who remained standing, framed by the internal porch light. 'All this talk of danger reminds me to tell you about the marsh on the island. It is behind the copse of trees near the fishing rocks. It's not very big but it can be a problem for those blundering into it. Sometimes you will see it as an obvious bog with standing water, other times there will be nothing much to it. The area should be marked with several two-metre red and white poles as a warning.'

'A real live challenge,' remarked Per. 'Who amongst us might lose their footing in the strange black bog?'

'Perhaps we need a traditional monster story instead?' said Erik. 'There is a cold sea around the island with plenty of water to hide a monster. Maybe we will see a Draugen on this trip.'

'What's a Draugen?' asked Mette. 'Is it a dragon?'

Magnus boomed from where he stood and raised his arms by his side. 'A Draugen is a giant man, covered in seaweed, who once drowned when out in a boat. The fishermen talk about him whenever there's a storm.'

'We do, it's true,' said Per, 'it's no joke. If the storm is bad enough then the Draugen will appear.'

'What does the Draugen do?' asked Mette. She was the only one who could look at Magnus at the front of the cabin.

'A Draugen comes back to kill the living,' said Magnus. 'He smashes the boats and drowns the fishermen.'

'Why does he do that?' asked Jonas. 'Is he a nutter?'

'He likes it,' replied Magnus, who had begun to scrape the top of his head back and forth on the ceiling, as if to scratch an itch. 'He likes to share his pain.'

'What an ugly monster,' said Jonas, also rising to his full height of six feet. 'Let's hope we have no storms around here.'

Magnus remained standing with head askew, arms now limp by his side, as if he had been hung from the rafters. He took the story on again. 'In some tales, a woman is chained to a post on the beach, where she is left to appease the Draugen.'

Linnéa whimpered in disgust, but Jonas wouldn't stop. 'The awful creature approached. He was seven feet tall, his face solid like yellow wax, with hairs sticking out of his nose and ears. He had yellow eyes, and an evil intent. His hands were impossibly large and calloused. The woman would rather die than become his plaything.'

'So she called out for help,' said Linnéa, 'but no-one came to save her, especially not the useless men who had courted her for weeks before.' She said the last *sotto voce*, but everyone heard her as intended.

'She called out to Sif,' boomed Magnus. 'Goddess of the Earth, wife of Thor.'

The cabin was silent. Magnus fully occupied the porch and looked like he had been stuffed there but didn't quite fit, he was so big. 'Sif,' she cried, 'burn me like a sheaf of corn, turn my dress to white ashes, and my body to black soot. Leave my dress on the beach as a warning to others. Bury my body in the marsh, where I might grab the ankles of men who dare to create these monsters.'

Suddenly, Mette shrieked. Per had clamped a hand on her leg. 'Don't! I'm scared.'

'Good,' said Erik, 'that's the point. Nice work, Magnus.'

There was a noise outside the cabin. 'What was that?' asked Linnéa. She looked wide-eyed out of the window.

'I don't know,' Erik said. 'A giant bluebird?'

'Professor! Come on, you heard it too,' said Linnéa. 'It sounded like an axe chopping wood.' She got up and went to the window for a look.

'Where's it coming from?' asked Mette. 'Is it close?'

They all listened and heard another distant thwack.

'That could be from anywhere, made by anything,' said Per. 'Sound travels a long way over water.'

Jonas stood up in the middle of the group as if he were in

charge. Erik was sitting back, watching him take over. 'I reckon someone on another island is chopping wood for the celebrations. It's Monday today. Midsummer Eve is on Saturday. I'm looking forward to the party. Can we build a bonfire?'

'Of course,' said Erik. 'We do so every year if the field trip coincides with Sankt Hans.'

They heard the cracking sound again. Linnéa was fearful. 'That sounds like it's nearby, maybe from up in the mountain?'

Erik watched the birds fly over the sea illuminated by the perpetual sun on the horizon. 'It sounds like the chopping of wood. Somewhere a traditional Norse is chopping wood ready to build a beacon or a bonfire.'

'I don't like it,' said Mette. 'It scares me.'

'I'll protect you,' said Per, putting his arm around her.

They all heard another sound and looked up to see Magnus grinding his teeth.

Linnéa turned to Erik. 'Will you protect us, Professor?'

'Of course he will,' said Mette.

Erik appeared touched. 'Of course. This island was claimed by my forefathers, and ever since then has been looked after by a Nordveit. It is my honour to carry on their good work and, like them, offer it protection. Even though things are different now, and much more comfortable, we are still in charge.' He sipped from his hot mug of spiced honey.

There was silence as they listened for more blows of metal axe splitting wood, or boulders on the mountain side calving into smaller rocks.

'The door is solid,' said Erik, 'the cabin is well timbered. We are well supplied.'

'But we have no communications!' said Linnéa.

'True,' said Erik. 'You will soon forget what day it is, and how long you have been here. You will return a different person to when you arrived.'

The lights on the room pillars went out and, in the gloom, a giant shape emerged from the cabin doorway. The figure walked between the students slumped on their cosy sofas. The contents of Erik's mug were spilt on the floor. He later said that it could have been much worse: Magnus' hands could have closed around slender necks in the half-dark. Students could have been carried away to their fate, two at a time, all the way up Trollveggen! At least Magnus would finally have been happy!

They all heard what Magnus whispered as he walked past Per. 'I want to stuff you into my sack.'

'Arsehole,' said Per, when the lights came back on. 'That's your monster, right there.'

CHAPTER 3

B ERGEN AIRPORT WAS clean, modern, well sign-post-
ed and easily navigated. I cleared passport control and
walked through the "Nothing to Declare" channel in Customs.
The Norwegian police officers were looking at me and one
called me over. He spoke English and I explained that I was
on my way to Ålesund and the art nouveau museum. Then
there was some serious squabbling in the queue behind the
policeman, so I was able to move on without having a conversation about where I was actually staying. Alexander Clearly
was going with the flow, as usual.

I took a tram to the market and looked around. The market
was full of customers browsing its stalls of fresh fish and other
seafood. Roasted whale did not appeal; the thick, dark meat
was an unnatural food to a visitor. Next to the dried, splayed
and butterflied fish were animal furs and hides everted from
eviscerated wolf, fox and reindeer. My hands ran over a wolf
skin: it was soft, silver and warm in the weak sun, the whole
pelt with the head still attached. I slung it over my back like
a cape and set the wolf's head upon my own head. The fangs
came down over my eyes. If I had a stick and a drum I could
be a shaman.

I took the wolf skin off and was going to give it back to
the stallholder when I noticed a bear appear in front of me,
a bear painted on the side of a metal hut. I stopped in my
tracks, noticing a door in the hut where a person could sit and

work. The bear stood on its hind legs holding a brush and a sign upon which was painted a single word: *Bjørnekrem*. The most powerful land animal in nature reduced to advertising shoeshine.

So why not wear the wolf skin and wear it with pride? This would be quite the fancy-dress; what great possibilities would come from this totem of virility and power? When needed in polite company, the head could be tipped back behind my neck. I raided the money my parents had given me and purchased the wolf skin.

The market holders worked quietly and efficiently. Knives flashed, sliced and slid fish off chopping blocks onto display boards. All around me this abundance of life was being laid out for its ending in a white bread roll. Fish fluttered in their holding tanks; then their heads were separated from their bodies and their guts pulled away from slowing muscles and arched spines. Flesh was pushed off bones with the back of a knife and scraped onto a board, and a sign denoting the price tag stuck in each fillet: fifty kroners for a sandwich that included some lettuce leaves. Then the board was dunked in water, run under a tap, and the process repeated by a member of the world's dominant species, the one wearing the orange plastic apron.

I wasn't hungry. I felt suddenly lonely; I was missing the warmth of Melanie and the excitement of our passion. But she needed rest, peace and safety; and most of all she needed her family. She didn't need me.

I left the market, patting the bear on its snout as I passed, much to the amusement of a woman selling plastic Viking helmets to tourists. It was a short walk to the harbour and when I reached it, I stood by the railings near where the fishing boats were berthed and thought about my next move.

Modern travel was easy. Getting to Bergen was easy. All you needed was your passport, some cash and to be prepared to wait a few hours at the airport for the next available flight. I knew that Ålesund was a minor destination, but it was enough to send me on my journey again. One destination was as good as another when all you wanted to do was travel; I had decided to hitch-hike and see the country that way. I now had a map of Norway that I had taken from the seat rest of the chair in front of me on the plane. Bergen was in the south, and there were a lot of roads, islands and fjords north towards Ålesund. The true north was well beyond, starting at Tromsø, according to the ancient adventurers.

Nearer the sea wall, several fishermen were working on boats at the end of wooden piers. They hosed the decks clean of the blood spilled by the fish now at the market, and loaded baskets and lines onto boats with red hulls and white decks. Some of the men were mending nets, talking loudly, mostly complaining.

A skinny dude with a white shirt hanging out over slim jeans slung below his hip bones tried to pick me up.

'English?' he asked, offering me a cigarette.

Was there a sign on my head? I took the cigarette and crumbled it in front of him.

He laughed. 'Yes, these cancer sticks are bad for you.' He lit up his cigarette. 'Where are you going?'

'I live here.'

'Really? What do you do?'

'I teach karate.'

He coughed and dropped his cigarette, caught it in his

hands, burnt himself. His smile was a mile wide. 'OK, I'll be careful.'

The fishermen were making a racket. 'What are they complaining about?' I asked.

'There are problems at the dam. Something has affected the salmon.' My new acquaintance listened on my behalf. 'The ferry company is not stopping along the coast until some problem at the harbour at Tromsø has been cleared up. Some of the men are saying to forget salmon and think about lobster instead.'

'Trouble in paradise,' I suggested.

'You think this is paradise. Have you seen my room?'

'I also teach kung fu.'

He looked at me sharply. 'You're different from the others.'

A seagull flew past my head, wheeled in the sky and landed on the mast of a fishing boat. Other birds followed, pecking at the litter on the ground. I cannot fly, so I will have to sail. I will have to be clever again. I will go up the coast and find Ålesund and enjoy it. Then I will move on and find a place to live for a while. I have three months I can spend as a tourist. Something tells me the people of this country will not mind me living amongst them. I can earn enough money to get by and I will be careful about whom I meet.

'Where can I get a boat out of here?'

'Don't you know? I thought you lived here?'

'I did once, but the neighbourhood's going downhill.'

'Screw you, tourist,' said my friend, and he walked away.

I found a newspaper stand and looked at the front page. Nothing in Norwegian made much sense. There were no English language papers on sale. I picked up the *Norway Post* and turned the pages. There was a large picture of a man wearing a strange pointed hat. He stood in front of a herd of reindeer with a rifle raised to his shoulder and aimed at a distant wolf.

I shivered, as if the wolf skin around my shoulders remembered the moment. Nothing was right in the world of the harbour fishermen, and there were other problems. The country was overrun with wolves, it seemed. Christmas would be threatened, owing to a lack of reindeer following their predations. I had jumped from the frying pan into the fire.

I walked around the harbour looking for a boat with a captain. Some of the fishermen I passed did not like my animal cloak: a man howled at me to make his point. So I wrapped the fur up around my arm and made no one else unhappy.

At one powerful-looking motor yacht, a dozen or more men were waiting. They were not fishermen, but climbers, kitted out in climbing gear. I heard some English words softened by French accents and figured that they were going up the coast to the next town. They seemed to be showing a lot of interest in the cliffs and did turn out to be some sort of mountaineering team.

A man with a white beard and a blue cap was doing the *Norway Post* crossword in the cabin of the boat. A sign on the quay said Taxi.

'Hello. Are you for hire?'

'What is your name and business?' asked the captain, not looking up.

'I am Alexander, son of Joseph, who married Harold's daughter, Margaret, both of the land of the Angles in the ancient times. My business is adventure.' I unwrapped the wolf skin and placed it back over my shoulders to make my point. 'Any chance of a ride to Ålesund?'

The captain looked at the fourteen men on the deck draped with ropes carrying hard helmets. 'Where is your gear?'

'They have my gear for me.'

'You do not look like a mountaineer.'

I leaned in. 'I'm the cook. Cordon Bleu. Usually do the chalets in the Alps. But for this season, I have the task of keeping this lot fed with haute cuisine.'

The captain shrugged. 'Fifty kroner.'

I pulled out the empty pockets of my trousers and placed my hands together as if I were pleading. Part of my brain acknowledged the comforting pressure of four hundred kroner strapped to my thigh.

'No.' The man shook his head and turned away. He put down his newspaper and walked past me to check on his paying customers.

I smelt the tobacco on the captain's breath and the wet wool of his jumper as he passed. My stomach tightened with the realisation that this would be the first of many tests. So I picked up the man's pen and newspaper and flipped through the pages until I found a full-page advert in which a lot of white space was wasted. Then I drew the man's portrait from memory with his pen.

The captain came back and was pleased with the likeness. 'And you cook?'

'I have some talents.'

I was allowed to join the fourteen men on board. One of them cast the boat off from the quay. The captain pressed a button in the cabin and started the engine. The boat moved out of the harbour into the main channel and steered a route between coloured buoys. The captain sought deep water away from the headlands. The fourteen men talked about climbing in the Alps. Their bogus cook kept out of the way while simultaneously managing to look as if he belonged. The sea became rough and the mighty fourteen fought to keep their food down. Gradually, the talking subsided. There were no heroics, just the sight of scum-flecked waves, as those brave men and I took turns to fight the monsters lurking unseen in the water.

The sun stayed above the horizon until the early evening and lit the way across the white-tipped sea. We made our way down a coastline split like the frond of a leaf into deep fjords. I felt optimistic about my new adventure. I had some hidden money, my passport, and a wolf skin over my shoulders. Best of all, I had free passage on what promised to be a beautiful trip to Ålesund.

CHAPTER 4

I N THE MORNING Linnéa and Mette headed out of the cabin first. They passed Erik, who was sitting at the main table. He was reading one of the papers in a mediocre scientific journal and nursing another mug of hot spiced honey. 'You're very keen,' he said, and then he noticed their dark eyes.

'Professor, how can we be expected to sleep with Magnus in the room?' Linnéa looked pained.

'Did he disturb you?' Erik was puzzled. 'He sleeps on the top bunk in the furthest corner, and none of the bunks next to him is taken. He is sleeping above me. He doesn't snore, or at least I didn't hear him snoring last night.'

'No, but I feel him watching me all the time, especially when I am undressing.' Linnéa looked at Mette, who agreed with her. 'He hides under his blanket and peeks out. I once saw his horrible yellow eyes peering at me when I had thought he was asleep.'

'We all have to get along, but if it's awkward for you, I can talk to Magnus and ask him to give you some space. Or perhaps you can change in the bathroom?'

Linnéa frowned. 'The bathroom is quite small. Really it is he who should move to a separate room,' she said.

'Where, exactly?' asked Erik. 'Where is this separate room?'

'I don't know. Under a table in the main cabin?'

'So we should treat him like a dog?'

Linnéa sighed. 'If he had any manners or social skills he

would let Mette and I change first in the dormitory, but we don't trust him not to come bursting in. There is no lock on the door.'

'I will ask Magnus to give you some space. I know he can be a difficult person,' said Erik quietly. 'He's a bit of a loner and rather awkward around people. Don't expect miracles from him.'

'I don't mind, to be honest,' said Mette. 'I've older brothers. We used to play naked when we were young. They taught me what to expect from boyfriends.'

'Eva, my daughter, says sometimes she wished for a brother as well,' said Erik. 'Apparently the experience would have prepared her in many wonderfully unexpected ways for romance and what have you.'

The young women pulled on their boots and got ready to head outside. Erik asked them to take some quadrats to the survey area from the pile he had stacked outside the cabin on the deck. A chill wind came hurtling through the cabin door as they left. He saw them pick up a few of the wooden square quadrats in each hand and walk away. Good, he thought. They were good students, keen to be getting on with it. The project was starting.

He was pulling the cabin door closed when Per and Jonas bowled into the main room. The young men were engaged in a mock wrestling match. Per had Jonas in a headlock, but Jonas had wrapped his long legs around Per and was pulling him over. They jogged the table as they fell past. Erik's mug of honey spilled some of its golden liquid onto the tablecloth.

'Be a bit more careful, boys,' said Erik. 'It's difficult even to get a drink in safety in this place.'

'Sorry, Professor.'

'Although I am glad to see you in such high spirits.'

'Slept like a lamb,' said Jonas. He looked out of the window and spotted Linnéa and Mette in the survey area. 'They're up and at it early.'

'They did not have such a good night. They found Magnus a troubling presence.'

'Yeah, he's gaseous,' said Per. 'They must have got hit by a couple of stink bombs.'

'I think I must be lucky,' said Erik, 'because as I get older, my sense of smell gets weaker.'

The young men moved to the kitchen, where Erik could hear the kettle burbling on the hob, and the sound of the toaster as it expelled warm slices of grilled bread. The generator kicked in with more power. He was pleased with how the cabin functioned now. Bø and Alfred would have been impressed by how it had evolved from a war-time shack. Erik turned back to reading his journal paper, which was on cadmium deposition in *Hylocomium splendens*, and, he had to admit, nothing special. His concentration was finally broken by the sound of Jonas or Per twanging the serrated breadknife on the edge of the kitchen table.

He overheard Per say to Jonas: 'Well done. You put Magnus in his place and he'll stay there now.'

The kitchen door closed and Erik could hear no more. He finished reading the paper and told himself he could have written a better article on the same topic.

Per and Jonas joined him at the table. 'Are you looking forward to your work today?' asked Erik.

'Definitely, this will be the year I crack moss reproduction. Never understood it before.'

Erik took a clump of moss from a bowl on the table and

squeezed it. Water dripped out of the sponge-like mass. 'Just as starters, and I know you know this, but remember that a moss has no roots. All it has are little rhizoids to attach to the substrate it sits on, be it rocks, tree bark, or whatever. So all of this water,' he squeezed out some more into the bowl, 'is from the air; and it includes all the nutrients the moss needs.'

He carefully pulled apart the moss and presented Jonas with a small green plant. 'Here is the gametophyte, with what looks like a stem and leaves." He handed over another, similar plant, which had a spore capsule on a stem growing out of the gametophyte. "This is the sporophyte which developed once sperm from the antheridium of a male gametophyte reached the archegonium of a female gametophyte. The sporophyte remains with the female gametophyte and relies on its nourishment."

'Of course,' said Per. 'I hope you're following, Jonas.'

Erik went on. 'Pollination is by dispersal of sperm in rain droplets. The sperm spreads about in the moss and fertilises the eggs in the female archegonia. After that, the capsules open and air dispersal takes care of the spores, which develop into protonemata and then gametophytes.' Erik smiled. 'Fascinating plants really.'

'Totally,' said Per.

'And what are you looking forward to on this trip, Per?' asked Erik.

Per looked down at his brioche roll.

'Come on, Per,' said Jonas, munching on some toast and jam. 'It's Tuesday, only six days to go, and then the next group will arrive on Monday. Just do the sampling, get some data, and I'll help you with the climate stuff. You'll be fine. Then you can join the navy or whatever it is you want to do.'

Erik frowned. 'It's a shame that no-one wants to be a botanist anymore.'

'There's no money in it,' said Jonas. 'It's interesting, but it'll never make anyone rich.'

'So you want to be rich?' Erik stirred the spoon around his cup and felt the heat transfer to the tips of his fingers.

'Of course I do. If I'm so smart, why can't I make money?'

'You sound just like my nephews, Jonas. OK. Go ahead. Work on the money markets, but watch out, it's not a nice life; very predator-prey.'

'I can handle it. I'm not as nice as I look.'

'It's true,' said Per. 'He's a man with sharp teeth.'

Jonas put on his boots and jacket. He waited for Per, who was now at the front door pulling on his yellow sea boots.

For a big man, Magnus could move quickly and silently. He had crept down the length of the cabin and into the kitchen before anyone noticed him. Soon they heard a strange keening that seemed to match the steam whistle of the kettle as it boiled.

'He's got problems,' said Per. 'He's a bomb waiting to explode.'

'He's just a little different to the average student,' said Erik quietly.

'Yeah, his skin's gone yellow for a start. Have you seen his eyes?' said Jonas.

'He has a medical problem related to his guts,' whispered Erik.

Jonas and Per went outside. A few minutes later Magnus emerged from the kitchen and took a chair at Erik's table. It was true that he did not look well. Erik stirred his mug of spiced honey and collected his thoughts. 'Good morning!' he said finally. 'How is Magnus today?'

Magnus said nothing. He just looked out of the window at the sea.

'Are you ready to start your project work today?'

Magnus turned to look at Erik with his terrible yellow eyes. 'Maybe?'

Erik felt the hairs on the back of his neck rise. 'What do you mean, maybe?'

Magnus swallowed whatever he was chewing with a noisy gulp. 'I'll do the work when I can, Professor. My head's killing me this morning. I can't concentrate. And you know that I am entitled to extra time in my studies.' Magnus looked out over the island with a smile on his face. 'I think I will go for a walk and see what this place is like.'

'That's fine, Magnus.' Erik said. 'Go for a walk. Enjoy the sights. Then come back and do some of your project work. Accomplish your goal and feel good about yourself. People will be proud of you.'

Magnus took a short-bladed switch knife out of his back pocket, flicked it open, and picked at his nails with the tip.

Erik didn't move. Magnus was close enough to stab him in the eye but Erik kept his nerve. He was dogged by this student who physically intimidated him as well as mentally wore him down. The mind behind those giant hands had already been called into question by events of a year ago. Magnus was taller and stronger than any of them on this trip. He had a history of suspected violence. Maybe attempts at rehabilitation were not so wise.

Magnus held up the blade of the knife to the window and watched the sunlight flash off the metal. 'You're obsessed with your work,' he told Erik with a sneer, as if the Professor suffered from some kind of illness.

Erik was taken aback. 'It's what keeps me young.'

'But what's the point of all these silly mosses. Do they make you rich? Do they get you women?' Magnus leant back in the chair until the wood creaked.

At least he is talking about his project, the reason for being here, thought Erik, and even he cannot destroy all the mosses. 'You're right, mosses are silly,' chuckled Erik, 'the lowest of the plants. You can't eat them, or grow them to make money, so you are correct, they will not make me rich. I agree with you, Magnus, mosses have been forgotten by many biologists. Well done for thinking critically about what you are doing.' He laughed again. 'But as luck would have it, most mosses are brilliant at capturing the pollution in the air. As you know, carpet-forming mosses derive their nutrients from wet and dry deposition. This makes the humble moss an excellent bio-indicator of airborne pollution. They pick up all sorts of heavy metals, and, most importantly, they are not affected by such contamination.'

Magnus pointed the tip of his knife at Erik, who kept his breathing regular as he looked death or serious injury in the face. 'I don't want a lecture.' He stood up, kicked his feet into his old boots, and walked out of the cabin.

Erik let out a long sigh of relief. Then he waved his hand in front of his nose and cried out. He literally ran out of the cabin to get away from the toxic pollution Magnus had emitted.

CHAPTER 5

W E HAD BEEN sailing for hours. I'd thrown up many times and been left at the side of the boat to survive as best I might by the captain. This was going to be a long dark night of the soul. I had the wolf skin over my shoulders and a leather satchel purloined from the mass of climbing equipment on the deck. The inside of the satchel was covered in white chalk. I was the least prepared adventurer ever, but I was improving my skill set. Other boats passed us, and in the distance a ferry moved slowly down the coast. What was I going to do after Ålesund? Go on a tour of the other avant garde museums in the country?

The sea heaved, and I heaved; it seemed about right. The back of my throat burned from the acid. The captain had the radio on. The music filtered out over the waves and calmed the sea. Then he pointed to a ragged group of tall islands on the horizon. It was a sight that grew more beautiful over the next hour. The captain pulled back on a lever in the wheelhouse. The action slowed the boat to a chug, and I was able to spot a jetty that I knew immediately was going to be my destination.

'Ålesund' said the captain, but I could see that it wasn't. It was a run-down fishing port that remained run-down, unlike Ålesund, which I knew had been rebuilt. Perhaps the captain didn't think I knew the difference. I wiped my mouth with the back of my hand. A couple of the climbers showed me the way down the gang plank and off the boat to the jetty. I was the naughty buccaneer about to be marooned. The penning of a group portrait of disgruntled climbers didn't seem on the cards, not when some of their gear and food was in the satchel hidden under the wolf skin. So I got off the boat and wished them well with a wave of my hand. The boat backed away from the jetty and turned back to the sea.

My legs regained some of their strength when once again I was on firm ground. Up ahead was a row of cottages on stilts amongst the rocks, their roofs grey, their walls orange. Behind these houses were the dark grey mountains streaked with snow and ice. Near the shore were three rusted poles sticking up about two metres out of the water. I wondered what they could be until it dawned on me that the poles were the masts of a sunken boat. There was a sign with a cartoon of an unexploded bomb. Get too near and then - boom!

That welcome was as encouraging as the welcome from the two men who watched me now as I walked into the unknown future. Where had the unkind captain dumped me? Was I being delivered as human cargo, intended for nefarious purposes in one of the most civilised, if underpopulated, countries on Earth?

I looked at my watch; it was nearly nine o'clock. I took a piece of paper about knots out of the satchel that I had found on the boat. I read it, studied it, read it again, and kept on going. The first rule of wandering about is always to look as if you know where you are going. I walked past the welcome committee without a stray glance towards them. I sucked in the clear, pure air. I was getting cold. When had I eaten last? The meal on the plane, I suppose, and that had only been a snack. With makeshift foresight I had borrowed the packet of peanuts from the woman sitting next to me, but those

34

peanuts were now floating ignominiously in the sea - or was it an ocean?

When I was some way past the men, having ignored them quite brilliantly, I heard modern dance music issuing from a radio in one of the huts. Two young women and a man were chilling out, eating something they were holding in their hands. Then the radio was switched off and the three of them departed, walking back to the quay.

They waved and said hello as they walked past. I waved back but was more absorbed in the task of tying a quick clove hitch knot on a karabiner. When I got to the house from which they had emerged I could see some food they had left on the deck. There was a small black grill with silver fish on top. One of the fish was still whole, the others were filleted and part eaten. There were bread rolls on a plate. I looked back and saw no-one was watching. I needed food and I needed somewhere to sleep. Of course, I could have turned around, introduced myself and made new friends of these people, later cadging some food from them. But then I knew there would be questions. I did not want any more questions to be asked about me, because I had asked them all already, back in England. Now I just wanted to enjoy being me, without any responsibilities.

So I crammed some of the fish into a bread roll and made off with it. The owners would barely notice the small morsels I had taken when they got back. The fish tasted all right, even if it appeared a little dark, and the bread was a rather stale; but I was hungry, so I ate the lot as I walked along.

Some steps suddenly appeared and I missed my footing. I stumbled and landed on the floor of a cabin-like structure that had loose fitting slats for walls. The cabin was suspended

35

high above the ground on immense poles. There was a hole in the middle of its ground floor, perhaps made for fishing, or more basic purposes. There was no evidence of fish, fish scales or skeletons, or indeed any smell of a creature, but only the sound of the lapping sea against the poles.

More people came into view, coming up from the quay, where a boat had just landed. I saw that the three people from whom I had stolen the fish were returning with friends. The newcomers all looked like tourists on their first excursion in a new place. They stopped at the house with the grill on the deck and stayed there. No-one saw me resting against a pole at the bottom of the fisherman's cabin, and I remained stock still, because the entire structure moved if I did. It wasn't safe, which was obviously why no-one else was there: if I could have read the native language I'd have realised that earlier. I then wondered if there were more unexploded bombs in the vicinity.

The cabin had another level, higher up, accessed via a pole. I hadn't climbed up a pole since I was eleven. It was in a PE lesson, my shoes tightly pressed against the cold metal, my arms straining from having to take my own weight. I climbed this pole now.

I made it onto the upper level, hooked my leg over the platform and rolled inelegantly inside. My trousers were now filthy, my hands red with rust and bleeding in a couple of places. To me however, the cabin offered an open invitation to come inside from the cold, and I had accepted it.

Not that I was the first to think of taking shelter there. In one corner I found empty vodka bottles, and elsewhere needles were lying, some still contained by and some now out of their protective sheaths. I was somewhat shocked by the sight; such squalor seemed inappropriate here, in the most pristine paradise in the world. I was also dismayed that I had wandered such a long way off the map.

I thought about my life in England: the house I had lived in, Mother and Father, my street, the demolished garage; and wondered if the houses had been built in its place yet. I remembered Mick and Melanie and the crazy stuff I got up to. I hoped that once my absence became general knowledge no one would take the opportunity to break into my house. I wouldn't be able to bear it if anyone damaged my recording equipment; it had taken such a long time to assemble. If I have no other claim to fame I am a sincere artist, dedicated to the cause.

And here tonight was the sincere artist's lot: a bare shelter that would offer scant protection from the frosty wind now tossing fat rain droplets inland.

I heard another noise, a light snuffling coming from the far side of the cabin. There was a gap between me and the man or woman who was lying there wrapped up in the dark green sleeping bag. I could have jumped whoever it was like a superhero, but that wasn't my style. I would have been more interested in drawing their likeness on the ground with a burnt-out stick of charcoal.

Outside, a party of young people were laughing and dancing down the street. One of the young women turned her head and saw me hunched high up in the disused cabin. She beckoned me over with a sly smile. I tasted fear at the back of my throat; felt my heart knocking at the ribs in my chest. A fine romance it would be, I thought; and no doubt some kind of trap.

I was shrunk in a corner hugging my knees to my chest. The wolf skin kept me warm enough. There was some protection up here from the wind and waves. Dinner was the remains of the fish sandwich and a bottle of water from the satchel bag. I had also taken some coffee biscuits, of all things, from the climbers and now I ate them for dessert. It was my first night in a new country and I had eschewed conventional accommodation in a hotel or hostel in favour of a more back to nature approach.

After a while, I began not to feel very well. The floor was hard but dry, so I curled up and tried to shake the feeling off. But when I tried to sleep, I was fighting an army whose soldiers were desperate to kill me. I was tightly wound inside my shirt and trousers, hugging myself, and the pushing and pulling of the enemy soldiers could not hurt me. Whenever they struck at me, I turned my shoulder, brought my shield up and thrust out my spear. They reeled back. There was crashing and the sound of waves as the attackers fell in the sea. I was with others who, just like me, were hiding, fighting, and surviving the onslaught. My brothers and I fought on brilliantly, one moment sheltering, the next moment standing up and attacking.

When I came to, if indeed I had been sleeping, the water was golden beneath me. I could not stop shivering. In fact I was shivering so hard I thought my ribs would break. My guts were rumbling and turning to water. I knew what was coming so I unstrapped the money belt around my right thigh and left it in the satchel. I reached the hole in the floor and shimmied down the pole to the ground. Just in time, I pulled down my trousers and boxers and squatted over the hole and, far below it, the sea, bracing myself for the violent explosion that followed.

Somehow I had picked up a fine case of food poisoning.

I was curious that I did not feel nauseous, although in other respects I felt I was turning into a biological weapon. My guts were destined to be a battleground for the next few days. The bottom had dropped out of my world. I needed clean water, some salt and some sugar for an oral rehydration solution.

Cleaning up was difficult and not very effective when performed with an old rag. When I got back to the upper level, the person in the sleeping bag in the corner had gone. Had they been so disgusted by my antics that they had run away? Then I realised the leather satchel had been tipped up: my money belt with passport and cash had been stolen. The thief had even taken the coffee biscuits but had left me a self-heating bag designed to warm up food. Ironical, under the circumstances, as I now had no food.

The shivering came on again; a great wracking of my body that caused pain across my chest and back. I crawled across the floor and got into the now-vacated green sleeping bag. My companion was many hundreds of kroner better off, and, morally speaking, could have had no cause for complaint about my reciprocal theft. I picked up the chemical heat-bag with a shaking hand. With my other hand, I poured into the bag some water from the bottle and sealed the top. I was reminded of the elephants I had made, especially the ones designed as gifts for Melanie towards the end of our relationship. I stuffed the steaming bag down my shirt and held it next to my heart. Curled in a ball clutching this and wrapped up in the stinking sleeping bag, I yet continued to shiver.

Well, this is another fine mess you've got me into, Laurel - or was it Hardy? No money, no passport, no food, no water. But you do have diarrhoea, chills, and dehydration. Was this the sort of vacation Alexander Clearly deserved?

Gradually the chemical heat pack warmed me up but the shivering grew only more intense. I wondered if this was the end of it all for me: I waited for the surging pain in my chest, the cessation of the rapid thumping of my heart. Was I about to finish my life in a deserted cabin on stilts above the Norwegian Sea, on some unknown island, a victim of youthful arrogance and ignorance, and more prosaically, gastroenteritis? Surely, I was too young to die?

I found that I was staring at the sun above the horizon, waiting for something to happen. The sea was escape, the land beyond yet to be discovered.

There was a second when everything stopped. The shivering stopped. My teeth stopped chattering. My heart stopped beating, or at least, if it was still beating, I was unaware of it. All external sensations stopped. It was a time when I could only wait, and it was bliss, absolute bliss. Any doubt that I was to survive, dissipated in the moment of the lightning strike that flooded over me and burned my brain. I relaxed completely. I was calm, serene, in harmony with nature. I was like Emerson incarnate; I saw all, I felt all, and I knew I would be fine. This ecstatic state was short-lived.

My muscles tensed and I slapped the wooden floor with the knuckles of my right hand. I began to bang the floor with my head.

CHAPTER 6

'ARE YOU OK, Professor?' asked Mette when Erik came running out of the cabin. She was standing on the deck, fixing the strings across a quadrat.

'I am now. Thank you, Mette.' Erik wiped his brow with his hand. 'Let's just say that Magnus could do with some education in personal hygiene.'

'It's not just his body that's the problem,' she said, 'it's his mind as well.'

'Yes, it's obvious there is a problem there, too. Anyway, Magnus has seen enough counsellors. The idea was to re-socialise him by letting him come on this field trip.'

Mette picked up another quadrat and turned it around on the deck to check that it was square. 'Is it true that he's been a student for twelve years?'

'Unfortunately, yes. It's a national record, and some say a national disgrace. He has had years of mitigation for various health problems, some of which you can guess at. But he has also had other excuses accepted. One year he even had an appeal upheld in his favour because an exam paper did not match closely enough the lectures he had downloaded, and he said that this put him at a disadvantage.'

Mette laughed. 'We never actually see him at lectures.'

'I'm not surprised. But now Magnus has finally acknowledged by signing that this is the final year of his studies.'

'And he gets to do the field trip, the one all the students

want to do, or used to.' Mette placed several quadrats on the ground in a neat pile. 'I was hoping more of my friends would want to come, but they all said no way, not if he's going to be there.'

'I'm sorry to hear that; putting off other students was always going to be a risk. So what makes you braver than them?' Erik strung another quadrat and put it on the top of the pile. 'That will cover the area.'

'I'm not brave at all,' laughed Mette. 'But you are here, so I feel safe.' She flashed him a sunny smile.

A good omen thought Erik. He had four fine students in his team, while only Magnus intended to be a thorn in his side. He would have to man-manage this problem carefully. He felt the power of his forefathers through the soil, through the silly mosses. He thought about what best to do with Magnus. If the recalcitrant student waved a knife at him again, he would find out who was boss.

It was ten o'clock by the time the students were ready to hear Erik introduce their projects. Jonas, Per, Linnéa and Mette all stood waiting outside the cabin, but there was no sign of Magnus. Erik fumed. He was the ruler of this island; it was his word that held sway. Erik's father, Alfred, would have tied the yellow giant's hands and put him on a boat for passage back to the mainland. His grandfather, Bø, would have shown him the cave he was so interested in, but also the drop into the sea behind the cave and the treacherous rocks. Great-grandfather Scyld would have dispatched him on the spot, making sure the body would never be discovered. But the latest descendant of the house of Nordveit was a calm and rational man, a liberal scientist, who made a point of giving everyone a chance.

'As you know, the mosses survey is performed every year. The last data showed us that the levels of cadmium, lead and mercury had all increased for the first time in twenty-five years. This was very surprising, but we have doubled-checked the results. They are correct; and they match those from other survey sites in the region.' Erik pointed to the ten-metre-high aluminium tower bedecked with meteorology instruments that stood next to the cabin. 'While this is a worrying development, at least we managed to get some funding for our new tower. Now we have accurate measurements of the relevant climate data, and we are part of a global climatology network.'

'So we can go home?' asked Per, who was standing near the tower and now patted it. 'This thing's doing a better job than us every day.'

'Not so fast, Per. The tower does not collect data on heavy metal deposition. We do that by taking samples of the mosses. We then measure the metal content by atomic absorption spectroscopy, back in the lab.'

'So what's the tower for?'

'Wind direction and speed is important, so we can calculate the likely source of contamination. Incident solar radiation is useful, as a measure of air quality. Air temperature and barometric pressure helps us to interpret weather patterns, and again the likely source of the pollutants.'

Jonas had his hand in the air. 'Professor, if we know that the air contains high levels of heavy metals, and we know that these are detrimental to human health, then why are we hanging around here without respirators or other safety equipment?'

It was the type of insightful question that Erik would have himself asked as a student. 'Good point, Jonas. The levels of heavy metal in the air are not acutely toxic. The levels are actually lower than those in certain industries, the making of glass products, for example, or residue from the burning of waste. But we suspect that the increase in metal contamination is the thin end of the wedge, and we need to keep track of it.'

'Where's it coming from?' asked Mette.

'The east,' replied Erik. They all looked out to sea, to the mainland of their home country, and then imagined a vast eastern land further inside the Arctic Circle.

'There's also something else, but it will not affect you because the work will be done back in the lab by my technicians. The samples this year will be analysed for organic pollutants. Mosses easily absorb pollutants, so this will be another great use for them.'

'What pollutants are we looking for?' asked Jonas.

'A great long list; I cannot remember them all. They are called POPS: persistent organic pollutants. One example is the family of polycyclic aromatic hydrocarbons.'

The students nodded. 'Do we get our names on any paper with our data, Professor?' asked Linnéa.

'Or just in the acknowledgments?' asked Jonas.

There was a time in years past when students would never have dared to ask such a bold question about a Professor's research publication practices.

'I'll do my best for you,' Erik replied. 'This year we need a more extensive sampling method. Mette, please survey the mosses around the cabin with quadrats.'

'Ok,' she said, 'I will be warmer here, and nearer the food in the cabin.'

'Jonas and Linnéa, please make a line transect, starting

from here and heading towards the boulder field. Measure and identify the species of mosses at every five metres. Now tell me, why are we using such a method for this, rather than quadrats?'

Jonas was first back with the reply. 'We anticipate more variation in the species of moss encountered because the landscape changes with altitude.'

'And also because the change in terrain makes the use of quadrats more difficult.' Linnéa was not far behind.

'Excellent!' To all his students, Erik said: 'Please do not tread on the mosses. We do not want to contaminate the samples with soil from our boots. Use the metal hooks to keep the quadrats in place or place a pole with a flag along the line transect.'

Per coughed discreetly. 'I know I'm not as smart as these guys, but I can still do something.'

'Per,' said Erik, 'I haven't forgotten you. Indeed, I have something rather special in mind.' He pointed over to the few trees on the island. 'This year I want to introduce a new development. We will take samples from the mosses on the trees. Cut your samples from the trunks and the branches, at one metre above the ground. You had better take your metre rule with you.'

Per brightened: 'This won't take long; there are hardly any trees on the island.'

'True, there aren't many, but one in fact is very special; maybe you have heard of it?'

The students looked intrigued.

Erik pointed to the copse where, amongst the firs, stood a shorter tree covered in white blossom. 'My wife and I planted an apple tree years ago, when we first realised Svindel had a future. This summer it has blossomed for the first time.' Erik shook his head. 'If ever climate change doubters needed evidence, they should come here. We transplanted it as a sapling from our garden in Tromsø. Marta and I are very fond of it.'

Mette was quite taken with the story. 'What a beautiful idea.'

'What about me?' said Magnus. He had approached them quietly from the cabin.

'Magnus,' said Erik, 'I have saved the best until last. This will be difficult, but I think you have the skills to do it. I would like you to take a grab sample every hundred metres or so. Start in the boulder field then go up Trollveggen as far as you can.'

Magnus looked up to the top of the mountain. 'You want me to go up there on my own?'

'Yes, please.' Erik edged closer to him and lowered his voice. 'The way is rough, hard on the feet. I don't think the others can really manage it. But I know that you can. Is that OK?'

Magnus was silent and Erik was sure he would refuse. He looked at his student with as much enthusiasm as he could manage. 'You can do this.'

Surprisingly, Magnus agreed with a grunt.

'You will need to drop a flag at every place you take a sample. It is an extreme form of line transect.' Erik reached into a canvas bag and pulled out some flags, red pennants on white metal poles with sharp pointed ends. 'You will need the sample bags as well.' He handed over a pack of sealable plastic bags. 'Place the samples in the basement freezer when you're done.'

Magnus pulled out a capacious dark leather sack from a

pocket in the back of his jeans. The poles, flags, and sample bags disappeared into it. He closed the neck of the sack with an enormous hand, slung the sack over his back, and set off. Magnus looked like a journeyman in days of old, walking though the countryside carrying his bag. He tramped off for the summit of Trollveggen as instructed.

Time passed. The island was a picture of grey rocks, green mosses, the golden cabin, all surrounded by the blue sea. The sky wore different colours throughout the morning, mauve to orange. Erik read a review that happened to praise his research; he agreed with everything the author said. Life was good. His students were at work, even though he couldn't actually see what Magnus was up to.

Erik had a nap in his deckchair on the porch. The students saw him fall asleep and immediately stopped work. They walked away from their plots and congregated just inside the boulder field. Jonas agreed to stand guard watching for the Professor to wake up. Linnéa and Mette stripped down to their bikinis, which they wore underneath their day clothes, and Per revealed a six pack and a hairy chest. They climbed up on to the boulders, laid their clothes down as blankets, and sun-bathed under the orange sky. The midnight sun hovered above the horizon, toasting their skin with faint warmth.

When Erik woke up he saw that all of the students were hard at work. He was impressed. Then he thought with some regret about a question that had bothered him. Was this to be his last field trip? He could retire next year and take life easy with Marta and Eva. Perhaps become emeritus on a sinecure with the university. Do a few lectures. Continue his research. See how much of an impact Svindel would have in the world of environmental monitoring after all.

Jonas and Linnéa were discussing their work when Erik came by. They asked for the password to the computer terminal at the rear of the cabin outside the dormitory. Apparently they had a sudden urge to check the temperature and precipitation records and copy them into their notebooks. Erik obliged, aware that mosses were not as interesting as the growing romance between two young people.

Erik next visited Mette, queen of a beautiful survey area made by twenty-five perfectly placed one-metre-square quadrats. Erik watched as she took the time to draw in her notebook each species of moss she encountered. A photograph would have been acceptable, but hers was an old-fashioned, tender approach, from someone who liked mosses as much as he did. There was indeed much to like about mosses, from their softness and ubiquity to the way they acted as a memory and a conscience of the planet. He watched as Mette stroked the back of her hand along the top of the moss carpet.

Erik was having a fine time. He was temporarily free from work and other interruptions. He was joyously relieved of the ups and downs of being head of department, and he had told the students about the resulting state of euphoria as he had landed the boat. No mobile communications for seven days was a good thing: they could all unplug from the twenty-four-seven world. But the students were already going cold turkey without mobile entertainment. He saw them checking their phones, and then when they couldn't get a signal they would put them away for the next fifteen minutes. Soon all the phones would be left behind in the dormitory, as they had been last year, and the students would transmute into less wired and more appealing versions of themselves. They would go back in time to when entertainment on the field trip

48

consisted of books, cards, telling stories, listening to the radio, and drinking beer.

Erik carried on his tour and went to check on how Per was doing. He headed for the fishing rocks, and soon was crunching over the smaller rocks, feeling the sea spray on his face. To his left he saw the earth darken around the swamp area. There was only one two-metre-high pole visible. He frowned; there should have been six poles warning anyone in danger of walking into the bog.

Per was standing by the branch of a fir tree when Erik found him. He was carefully removing a layer of moss with a small blunt knife and placing it into a plastic sample bag. It was evidently his first sample.

'Where is your log book, Per?'

'I've made some notes on a bit of paper.' He pulled out a crumbled sheet from this pocket.

'You need a log book. Loose pieces of paper get lost or ruined.'

'OK, I'm sorry.'

Erik spied a fishing rod set down on the rocks near the shore. 'How's the fishing?'

It was possible that Per was blushing, just a little, in the area around his ears. 'It will be fine, but I need some good bait. Fish don't like moss.'

'I actually didn't know that, Per. Thank you for adding to my favourite information store.'

'You're welcome.'

Erik walked a few yards to the apple tree. Against all odds, including a wager against him from his colleagues, his humble example of *Malus domesticus* had survived transplantation from the mainland and was now thriving on Svindel. Was there anything prettier than apple blossom? He didn't think so. Carefully he pulled down a branch and let it go again. It sprang back up with youthful vigour. To see his and Marta's tree bear fruit would be the next challenge.

Back in the cabin, Erik brought up supplies from the basement, restocked the kitchen, and prepared a picnic lunch for everyone: bread, cheese, apples, and small packs of salami. He joined the students outside on the deck where they ate and looked out across the island. The sea rippled peacefully, and the breeze blew lazily. They drank water from china mugs and watched the world go by.

'This is more like it,' said Jonas.

Per agreed. 'Yep, he's not here, and we all benefit.'

Linnéa shook her head. 'Please don't mention him. He gives me the heebie-jeebies,'

Mette suddenly piped up. 'Professor, are there any herbs or flowers growing on the island?'

'Herbs or flowers?' queried Erik, as if he were deaf, although at this time of year he was well aware of why a young woman might be interested in finding herbs or flowers. A mixture of seven was the usual quantity. 'There is the very lovely *Dianthus superbus*. You might find it on the higher ground above the rocks where Per is fishing.' He turned to point to exactly where he meant. 'It likes a well-drained soil, and in that area the water runs off into the rocks. It is known as 'Fringed Pink' and is quite a delicate flower.'

Then he got more serious. 'But you will also see in that area *Veratrum album*, which is white hellebore. It is a tall plant with attractive white flowers that have some ornamental value. However, please take care: all parts of the plant are poisonous.'

He spread his hands wide. 'Apart from those two, I think that's it.'

Mette thanked him.

'Is this for a business idea, Mette?' teased Jonas.

Mette nodded. 'Floral aerosol sprays for pillows and bed-sheets,' she said, 'a different blend for every occasion.'

Erik was just thinking what a good idea Mette had come up with, when they all looked up at the sight and sound of something crashing down towards them.

CHAPTER 7

W HEN I CAME to, I was lying prostrate on the floor of the filthy shack. I had such a headache. Had I been mugged? Had I been hit on the back of the head? I also heard laughing. Was that my mugger? I stopped when I realised it was me who was laughing. I turned over and got up slowly. There was no blood when I inspected the back of my head with my hand. My face felt strange, as if I had been in a gurning contest. I checked that I had all my teeth.

The familiar pounding was back in my chest. My heart was beating uncomfortably again; but I really was lovely and warm. The yellow and purple flowers of some underwater plants, which were growing up the pole, brightened my day. I marvelled the inhospitable corners where life proved it could survive and flourish; I hope it regarded me as a promising specimen, too.

I slept for an unknown time. My brothers-in-arms protected me with their shields. I was ready to spring into action with my spear if anyone invaded the cabin. But no-one arrived, and the owner of the sleeping bag did not return.

When I was ready to move, I made a checklist. I needed a litre of boiled water with eight teaspoons of sugar and one teaspoon of salt. The recipe for an oral rehydration solution was just about the only thing I remembered from school biology, perhaps because it had a practical dimension. Eventually I would need food, but not too soon, or it would reappear at the furthest end of the unspeakable tube. My clothes were even more disgusting than the sleeping bag, which defied belief. I had a leather satchel and I wore a wolf skin. All I needed now was a quest with a defined end and I would be on my way.

My balance was so bad when I got up, and I felt so light-headed when I tried to walk, that I was obliged to move about on my knees. In doing so I uncovered a useful find, a polished wooden object with metal ends. When I pressed on the button in the handle a slender, tapering blade of about four inches in length shot forth. I closed up the knife and put it in my trouser pocket. My egress from upstairs was a quick slither down the pole to the ground, after which I stumbled up the steps away from the dilapidated cabin. I was standing shakily on the road again, the wolf skin wrapped around me and the satchel over one shoulder. I resembled the star of a disaster movie.

What day was it? What was the time? It was bright all around. Was it morning?

Where exactly was I? Where was I going? What silly questions. The answer was onwards, of course. The adventurer moves on, to explore, to discover, to witness. The adventurer moves on with proper regard for his health, environment and those in it. I knelt down and cupped both hands in the sea. The water was ice cold and I held my breath when I splashed my face. I stood up, somewhat energised, but realised I had a long way to go, and my guts were already turning to liquid again.

Some fresh water to drink would be very welcome, as would some plain bread. I was glad the thief had taken the coffee biscuits. Some distant memory told me that sweet food fed gut bacteria and made diarrhoea worse.

I walked slowly along the only road in the village, moving inland towards the collection of houses. A woman was standing on the side of the road. She was shorter than I and had a shock of snow-white hair. She asked me a question.

I stopped and mimed drinking, an action which I immediately regretted. She would think that I was a drunk and needed alcohol. I cast about for the Norwegian word for water. I tried "wasser" and "aqua" and put my hands over my abdomen.

She pointed to a church that was at the end of the island, framed in front of the mountains.

I clasped both hands together and bowed, then headed for the church. As I walked, I took deep breaths of cold air into my lungs. Before long a familiar but unwanted sensation welled up. There was a path off to the beach, and some secluded rocks. I took off the wolf skin just in time. The moment my trousers were around my ankles, the world fell out of my bottom. I figured I had two or three days of this to endure, then another two while I recovered. This time next week I would be laughing.

I kicked sand over the devastation I had left and looked around. No one was about. I stripped off and walked into the sea. When I was clean, I walked back to the rocks, dried myself with my trousers, and slung the wolf skin over my shoulder with the head in position on mine.

In the foyer of the wooden church was a man wearing a blue hat. His face was weathered and tanned like an old leather bottle.

'English?' he asked.

I looked at him. How did he know?

'Shouting. Fighting.' A man appeared out of the gloom of the dark door behind him. 'Bernt heard fighting.'

'Sorry,' I said. 'I had a funny dream.' I looked at Bernt. Was he the owner of the green sleeping bag?

The door-warden smiled. 'Come in. Get warm. Eat, drink. Sleep one night.'

I was happy to take up his offer. Inside the church I saw the red, black and white of the Norwegian flag. There was also the plain red-on-white of the Red Cross.

On a wooden trestle table at the back of the church another snow-haired woman served bread and slices of cheese that had been set out on a plate. She tended a saucepan heating gently on a camping stove. When the food was ready, she ladled out a mug of a dark brown meaty broth and gave it to me.

'Aqua?' I asked.

'Vann,' she said. The woman produced a plastic pitcher of water. She poured it into a white coffee cup on the side of which was advertised the services of my old friend *Bjørnekrem* the shoeshine. The coincidence was comforting. I drank three cups of water, or vann, and filled the cup a fourth time.

Was it too early for a meat broth? This was an easy question to answer, because what else was I going to eat today for breakfast? I accepted the cup of broth and took a seat at the nearest table. One sip of the salty, scalding liquid woke me up and changed me into a better person. The bread was hard and dark, made of rye I supposed, and it needed plenty of chewing. The cheese tasted of nothing at all. As I ate, I wondered about all the earlier silliness: the striving, the synaesthesia, all that watching myself from afar. It was so good to be able to give it all up, and so quickly and completely, too, and start again.

A shield hung on the wall, patterned with a tangle of curled lines representing a tree and a snake. The head of the snake gave out fire. I took it all in, warming to my abandonment as the meat broth warmed my body.

There were flashing lights outside and I heard the voices of at least two men talking to the door warden. The bread and cheese went into my satchel. I placed the mugs of water and broth under the table, out of sight. I was in the shadows at the end of the church by the time the three policemen entered the nave.

They wore black jackets with badges: their insignia depicted lions wielding axes. Three of them, I thought, how exciting, but they would not catch me. The policemen spoke with the woman serving the food and she pointed to the table where I had sat. One of them walked over and soon found where I had been sitting. In a flash I was out of the far door, following Bernt, who didn't fancy a conversation with them either.

There wasn't much cover outside the church. I was looking for somewhere to hide when a stone flew over and landed in front of me. Bernt popped up from behind a wall and I went over to him. He pointed at a car on the road. The passenger door was open. The exhaust smoke curled up into the air.

'Thank you,' I said. 'Takk.'

He ran off before I could question him about the previous night. I was in no state to chase after him, to wrestle back my passport and money, if indeed he had them. I shuffled quickly to the car and got in. The driver was a man of about my age, European-looking, with a beard. 'We go to Vestvågøy. OK?'

'Oui, c'est bon,' I answered.

He looked at me with surprise. Presumably Bernt had told him that I was English, but you know me, I never like to be pinned down.

I got in, closed the door and he drove off. There was no

activity in the rear-view window. I didn't see any policemen following us, not that I really needed to worry, but the idea of an adventure had gripped me. After five minutes it was clear that my driver did not want to talk much, so I took the bread and cheese out of my satchel and finished it off.

There was a map sticking out of one of the cup holders. 'Puis-je?' I asked. He nodded. The map unfolded to show the islands in the area. I looked at it long and hard, and my friend pointed his finger at our location. As a result I immediately found Vestvågøy.

'Merci pour le trajet.' I reached out my hand. 'Je suis Jean.'
'Morten. Bonjour.'

CHAPTER 8

A S SOON AS he was up on the steeper slopes of
Trollveggen and hidden from view, Magnus took out
his sack and dumped all the flags, poles and plastic bags in the
rocks. Then he headed upwards, on the look out for Bø's cave.

The path up the mountain had sloped gently upwards at
first, but once he'd left the field where the giant boulders
rested after their travels down the hill, Magnus had to face the
challenge of progressively steeper inclines to the top. To his
right was an almost vertical wall that led into what looked like
the source of the boulders, there were so many scattered about.
Even if he did get over that obstacle, the next section was
similar, but with some even more hostile angles to conquer.
Magnus considered going back and trying a less steep route
by starting nearer the fishing rocks. This would nearly lead
him to the copse of trees where Per worked. It would also
take him to the swamp, which suggested to him all sorts of
interesting possibilities. But a troll marches straight up a hill,
and no less a man than Professor Nordveit had told Magnus
to go up and take Trollveggen.

So Magnus chose to go left and turn into a slight hollow
in the wall, where he stepped over a few boulders; and, calling
on his greater than average height and strength, he managed
to scramble up to a plateau. Here, a whole army of boulders
was waiting to fall on his head. He crawled past them until
eventually he was able to stand up and look down at the cabin.

The students were sunbathing on the rocks: Linnéa and Mette were in their bikinis; Per was shirt-less next to them. Jonas was standing on the tallest boulder, looking up the mountain. The Professor was sitting in his chair on the deck.

Magnus walked around the edge of the high plateau. One slip, or one step out of place and he would be over the edge, falling straight down into the sea. White seabirds flew up and around him as he edged towards the windy northern side of the island. The wind seemed to gather speed around the cliffs and he dropped to his knees so as not to fly away with the birds. He watched the waves surge up and then recede away from a group of rocks. It looked like the sea was breathing, perhaps waiting for him.

Trollveggen, or the troll wall, was well named. He had respect for Grandpa Bø if he had come up and down this route every day. Even if the boulders had shifted somewhat from the old man's time, the underlying terrain was very steep and difficult. There was a trickle of yet more boulders in front of Magnus, falling away from the crumbling summit. Magnus paused. To his right he saw the start of an enormous depression in the cliff face, as if a much larger troll had stood in the sea and pushed in the side of the cliff with its thumb.

He edged as far along the cliff edge as possible before coming up against another wall. He poked out his head for a look around the corner and saw that he was now above the cave. A few metres below lay a narrow ledge of moss-covered rock. There was no way forward and there was only one way back. But he had found the cave as instructed, so his next move was forced upon him. He turned around and lowered himself down the cliff until he was fully stretched, with his legs dangling in the air above the ledge. His arms started to burn with the effort of holding his body weight. If he dropped and missed the ledge, he knew he would end up in the sea or lay broken on the rocks thirty metres below.

He let go. His boots hit the ledge and when he felt the pain shoot through his knees he immediately bent his legs and tipped his body forwards. He flailed out his arms, searching for something to grip. He grabbed on to the rocks, which were slippery with bird droppings, and held on. A loss of balance here would mean a backward dive on to the rocks. The roar of the sea added to the roar of the wind as his fate was decided by the laws of physics. He was lucky to make it from the ledge to the safety of the cave entrance. The wind whipped up around him but could not evict him now – he was inside the cave.

What he found did not disappoint him. For the first time in a long while Magnus felt joy and happiness surge through his heart. It was a magnificent cavern, with white walls and a high wide ceiling of white stone. He walked around and marvelled at the place. There was a small pit worn into its floor, fashioned by the heat of many fires. Up above was a natural rock chimney with daylight showing at its top. He looked again. It was a very wide chimney, one that a man could traverse with his back against one wall and his feet against the other. That must have been the way clever old Bø would have come in and out. As an entrance it would have been easy to defend: imagine peering down at Bø and his sharpshooters! And of course, the chimney would have ventilated a fire very nicely. The fire pit was not situated directly under the chimney, so if rain fell into the cave the fire would still burn. It was time to test his theory and make a fire himself. By doing so he could tell the world that Tollveggen had fallen to Magnus the Great.

The cliff edge was streaked white with droppings from the birds, slippery new mess slithering on top of old guano. There were several nests of various shapes and sizes, the largest about the size of the shopping basket on a bicycle. He brought this nest inside, admiring the artistry of the birds, and then dismantled it, sorting piles of twigs of different sizes for tinder. He had come well prepared to light a fire. He took out the magnesium fire starter, which accompanied him everywhere he went, together with some handy items he had stolen from the cabin. Linnéa and Mette might even now be asking who had stolen their cotton wool and what had happened to a jar of petroleum jelly.

Magnus smeared a ball of cotton wool with the viscous jelly. He pulled the ball slightly apart, checked it was still dry inside, and set it down on the dry floor of the pit. He scraped the flint along the fire starter, producing a shower of sparks. The cotton wool ball caught fire and a flame rose up. It was a sight to behold. His mouth widened into a smile. He placed the smallest twigs, thinned by splitting them down the middle with the nail of his thumb, over the burning ball. He held his breath: the dry wood caught and the flame grew higher and stronger. The next size of tinder, twigs the size of matchsticks, was equally lovingly applied; the flames lapped hungrily at the wood and grew higher. The swirling smoke gathered and rose in a visible grey column that curled towards the chimney-hole. The fire was small; it would not last long, even if he burnt all of the bird's nest, but at least it warmed his hands. Best of all, it was a beacon, a presage of things to come.

When his stomach cramped and his guts rumbled, Magnus

thought about food. He had found Bø's cave and he would come back here, that was for sure. For now, he needed to bring in supplies.

He also needed to test his idea that the smoke was leaving via the main entrance and exit to the cave. He squeezed into the chimney: it was a tight fit for him; it would have been more comfortable for a man of normal size. He pressed his back into the wall behind him and placed his right foot on the opposite wall. He pushed with his right leg but got nowhere. Then he brought up his left leg underneath him and straightened it when he pushed again. Up he rose by a few inches. Emboldened, he repeated his movements, refining them until he rose higher and quicker. Certain footholds suggested themselves, depressions in the opposite wall where boots had pressed before.

It took him a couple of minutes, but eventually he was moving up the chimney towards the light. This was turning into one of the best days of his life. He had found Bø's cave – he couldn't believe it. This sort of thing didn't happen to people like him. He counted eleven footholds on the opposite wall, and he learned to alternate the leg he used to push up with until he was moving with a fluidity that he found exhilarating. The light came nearer until his head emerged into the noise of the wind on top of the mountain. He climbed out of the chimney, wreathed in smoke from the little fire below, and stood up surrounded by boulders. They were the ancestors of those who had fallen and stumbled down the mountain side. He held up his arms to the sky and yelled into the wind. Watch out world! Here is Magnus the Great! Here is the King of Trollveggen!

For the chimney to be a reliable entrance and exit to his

cave (it was Bø's cave no longer) he would have to shift a few of the large rocks out of the way. Magnus pushed at a boulder that reached his waist; it stood intransigent, overcoming the force he applied. He positioned himself behind the boulder and pushed hard at it with his dilapidated boots, their condition worsened by the climb up the chimney. The boulder rocked slightly and, under pressure from his continued effort, rolled towards the cliff edge. Magnus stood up and observed its fall from the cliff. After a couple of seconds of silence, he heard the boulder enter the sea with an enormous splash. The column of water that it produced sprayed upwards to where he was standing. The droplets hung in the air in front of his face like frozen rain. Then the spray plummeted to the sea again.

He smiled. This was the best fun he'd ever had. He kicked and shoved at other boulders around the chimney hole. They, too, bounced and fell off the cliff edge and splashed into the sea. After several minutes' hard work he was panting, but feeling very good. Exercise always made him feel better. Cooped up in that cabin with people he didn't like was a sure way of boring him to distraction.

The area around the chimney hole was clear of boulders that might obstruct the only means of entrance and exit. He peered down through the chimney and his eyes were stung by the few wisps of smoke. The bird's nest was consumed by fire. Climbing down into the cave would be quite a feat, and one which he would practise on another occasion. His fun was nearly over for the day, but not quite.

The King of Trollveggen stood on the summit and stared all the way down the mountain to the golden cabin surrounded by the green carpet of mosses below. It had no magical ring of protection. He pushed at a reasonably large rock, about the size of a dog. He moved it easily, and sent it skipping downhill, increasing in momentum until it sprang up into the air as if it were a pursued rabbit. The rock ran purposefully in one direction for several skips, then as if in surprise changed direction, pursuing another course until it finally lay, spent, at the head of the boulder field.

He saw the students looking up at the mountain, so he kicked larger and larger stones downhill and watched the falling missiles scatter and shoot around the boulder field in front of the cabin. The students backed away from the freak landslide but remained near the cabin.

Magnus selected the largest boulder he had thought he possessed the strength to move. He stood behind it and shoved at it with his boot. The boulder reached his shoulders and was weathered on one side, like a giant's toenail. It moved very slightly, then rocked back into position. He leant his shoulder against it and gave the boulder a massive, arm-wrenching shove. The enormous rock moved again, teetered on its fulcrum, and disappointingly fell back into place. Magnus took a deep breath: this was going to hurt. He walked back a few steps, then suddenly stepped up to the boulder as if about to kick down a door. He planted his left leg solidly on the ground as support, and at the same time kicked out at the boulder with his right leg. It was like kicking the mountain itself, but he kept shoving and pushing at the immense weight until he had beaten the inertia of the boulder and sent it rolling down the hill. The boulder turned over and over as it descended the mountain side. It was heading straight for the cabin.

The students and their Professor ran. They scattered like seeds from a pod. It was quite the most wonderful thing Magnus had ever seen. The boulder leapt into the middle of the boulder field and cannoned into an equally large boulder lying in front of the cabin. The indomitable force of the moving object crashed into the stationary stone with a clap like thunder. Slivers of stones exploded into the air. It was an aerial bombardment any enemy would have been delighted with, and best of all he could pass it off as a freak accident of nature! He watched as the Professor and the students fled for their lives towards the southern shore behind the cabin.

They were still hiding when Magnus the Great strode into town. He walked with a giant's stride, up and over the boulders, jumping from the top of one to another. Dressed in his black designer coat, he ignored the cowering students and their Professor, and walked straight into the cabin.

CHAPTER 9

MORTEN AND I drove through the night. We must have covered hundreds of kilometres. None of the places marked on the road signs meant anything to me: Trondheim, Steinkjer. The name Vestvågøy rang a bell. A northern paradise, pretty beaches? We would see. We crossed the bridge to an island and carried on. At one point we saw two young women standing at the side of the road. Morten shook his head and wouldn't look at them. The car was a two-seater; they couldn't have squeezed in if they'd tried.

'J'ai faim. J'ai besoin d'un lavage.'

Morten grinned. 'Oui, moi aussi.'

We said nothing else for a while as the road cut through the island between modern houses and away from the fishermen's cabins further out near the coast.

We passed a Sami trader standing at the side of the road. The sign above his long wooden shed read 'Spekemat'. Morten looked pleased and pulled over.

I got out of the car. My eyesight dimmed for a few seconds and then readjusted itself. I needed food, water and rest. I knew that we were travelling north and that was fine by me, but I still had no clue where I was heading.

The stall was very colourful; the flags of many countries were displayed on its roof. Several large sets of reindeer antlers stood by the side of the wooden shack. A small reindeer was tethered out the front.

The trader sold cured meats - salamis and pepperonis - and not much else. I asked for aqua, then vann, and the trader produced a half litre bottle. He demanded twenty kroner.

I would have liked to have written a postcard home asking for the money to be wired over, but we all knew that wasn't going to happen. Home seemed a long way away, and many years ago.

Morten stepped in and bought two bottles of water and some salami, which seemed to be a favourite of his, and asked for bread in French and then English.

'Je dois pain et d'eau.' Morten handed me a bottle of water and bread roll.

'Merci. J'ai faim.' The smell of the salami was making me light-headed.

Morten saw me looking at a rack full of sweets and crisps. I eyed up a bag of popcorn like a kid. Salted, sweet popcorn was just what the doctor ordered, washed down with a bottle of water. That would get rid of the bugs living it up in my intestines. But I had no money. I had the clothes on my back, which stank to high heaven, and a wolf skin over my shoulders. My new friend, Morten, was giving me a long lift north into the country. Why? Out of the goodness of his heart? Was I well enough to be making such a journey?

We settled down by the car at the side of the road. Morten offered me some salami, but it smelled so strong and looked so rich and fatty that I declined it. Bland bread and cool water were what I needed.

A phone appeared in Morten's hand. He held it up and took a picture of me. Was this it? Was this to be the last recorded image of Alexander Clearly?

If I had a phone myself, I would be able to call for help.

The number for the emergency services was 112. I felt safe knowing this little fact. But I had brought no phone, not really being a fan of them, and of course I had nothing else that could help me, apart from my wits.

Morten unfolded the map he'd taken from the car. He showed me roughly where we were, just south of Bodø. He was heading for the ferry from a point west of Bodø to the Lofoten islands. Did I want to come?

I took stock of the situation. The alternative for Ålesund, where I had been dumped, was a long way south and a lot had happened since I'd been there. Thoughts of art had receded. Thoughts of survival predominated. I had no money. I had some skills, but I needed people to work them on. I needed to meet or entertain a certain type of person, one with an interest in the finer things in life and a good disposable income. So I needed a city, a cosmopolitan centre where I could work my magic, or at least survive by practising the arts. It didn't sound like I needed an island peopled by young travellers and tourists who would be careful with their cash, always looking for a good deal.

So I shook my head and pointed north to Narvik and Tromsø. These were large cities, large enough to supply what I needed, but Tromsø was a long way further north than the Lofotens. I saw that Morten was not interested in making such a detour. Instead he agreed, with a shrug, that he could drop me at Saltstraumen or Straumsnes, small places on the map inland of Bodø but still on Route 80 heading north.

I urinated at the side of the road, the reindeer watching me, and climbed back inside the car. We set off again and within five minutes I had realised that the bacteria in my guts were thanking me once again, churning away to create gas and fluid.

We drove past a petrol station where a man was standing outside watching the traffic go by. I looked for Mick and Ying, and then just shook my head. Morten gave a little laugh too, but for other reasons. He explained it was because on his way down south yesterday he had passed the same serious-looking man as he began his vigil outside the petrol station. 'Vingt quatre heures!' he said, looking at his watch.

It was a very nice watch. He was generous with his money. I wondered what he had been doing down south. How come he had ended up outside the Red Cross mission on the unnamed island I had been dumped on? His French was as bad as my own. Stress began to leave red marks on my forehead and at the back of my neck. My imagination got into gear.

We passed through Saltstraumen. A sign for Bodø appeared. I followed along on the map as we went through Løding and expected a right turn along Route 80 to Straumsnes. But Morten slowed and turned left towards the coast. Had he forgotten what he had agreed to do? He looked tired and he didn't notice me scrutinising him. I noticed he wore his cap in the car and wondered about his hair. His beard was mid-brown but his hair was darker. I enjoy a bit of dressing up as much as the next man, but you must do it properly.

The next road sign was for Bodø; and the next for the ferry to the Lofotens. One look at the map showed that these islands were long, and no doubt beautiful, but they were not a suitable destination for me. Yet we passed through Bodø and headed for the ferry. I had expected the car to slow and let me off before Bodø. Had Morten completely forgotten he'd promised this? I needed to stay in a place with lots of people: I didn't want to be stuck on an island or captured at a ferry terminal, where I knew there would be police and border agents and the like.

Morten looked straight ahead as he drove. Suddenly I really did not want to be in this car at all: I wanted to follow the route on the map and head north. I was sick and angry. My guts went cold and my heart rate quickened. My mouth was dry. This felt wrong: where were we going?

I began sighing, and breathing deeply, running my tongue around my mouth. 'Qu'est-ce que c'est?' he asked?

I held up my hand. 'Ralentir.' It wasn't hard to feel sick under the circumstances. We were in a lightly populated area on the outskirts of Bodø. Morten slowed down. I was about to get robbed and left, destitute, on the side of the road. He would escape on the ferry to the Lofotens. I saw his plan now.

'Médecine,' I groaned. There was a plastic shopping bag on the floor of the car. I held it open in front of me. Morten swore and pulled over. He got out of the car and walked around the front of it to my side. I shivered, cold all over from fear and adrenaline, half-ill, half-feigning illness. Reaching over, I removed the key from the ignition.

Morten pulled open the door and I stumbled out, holding the bag into which I had stuffed some bread and a bottle of water. I was taller than he, although he was stockier. He was in good health, though, and I was in fact quite ill. If we had a fight, there was only a fifty-fifty chance I would win.

I drew out the knife I had found in the tumbled-down cabin.

'Merde,' he said, backing away. He stammered, trying hard to find the English to question me. 'What are you doing? You are not so ill now.'

Two young women cycled past carrying tents on their

bikes. I hid the knife out of sight. I couldn't believe that I had threatened Morten with it, but I had to protect myself.

I walked backwards down the road, keeping Morten in sight the whole time. When I was far enough away, I threw the car key back to him. The silver key on its black fob landed in front of him on the road. He stuck two fingers up to me, got back in the car and drove off towards the ferry. I certainly was not going to the islands now.

Four more cyclists rode by, a middle-aged group. They took some notice of the vagabond at the side of the road wearing the wolf skin but did not disturb me. It was a very peaceful place for placid people to walk or ride their bikes or drive their cars. The lone Englishman, the one with the knife, if Morten reported the incident to the police and the newspapers, was spotted earlier on the road to the Bodø ferry terminal. No doubt there would be police circling in a helicopter overhead or driving towards me very soon.

What had happened beggared belief, but at least I had escaped and was still in charge of my own destiny. I folded the knife away and put it in my pocket. There was some bread and a bottle of water in the bag, and half a salami sausage that looked so revolting I threw it into the woods. But I was too late; even the sight of it had plunged my intestines into catastrophe again. Within minutes I was squatting behind a tree far away from the road, my guts heaving. Drink fluids, I thought, amid the devastation. Add some sugar and a pinch of salt. The water will rehydrate your blood and the bacteria will be swept from your intestines.

I used most of the bottled water to wash myself clean. In my need for a towel I sacrificed my shirt, after which I buried it under some leaves. It had become so soiled that even a professional laundry could not save it. I did up my trousers, stood with the wolf skin wrapped over my shoulders and gathered together my wits. I needed the basics: fire, shelter, food and water. The country was unusually warm during the day, but at night the air was cold. Clothes could be found or purloined on the sly. Water was a priority but any house or business would offer some opportunity. A bit of food would be welcome; snacks would be the easiest to steal. A warm shelter would leave me no worse off than those cyclists camping in their tents on the islands.

A passing car slowed down to have a look at me standing on the side of the road. Obviously there was a reporter inside beaming his story straight back to the newsroom. The Englishman who liked to wear the wolf skin was spotted in the evening on the road walking away from the Bodø ferry terminal. He is presumed to be heading north, having threatened at knife point the driver of a car who he met in the south. Members of the public are advised not to approach him but to call 112.

My plan was to walk up the road and head inland the way we had come in. I would flag down someone driving away from the ferry terminal and hope that they were heading north to Narvik. I waited for another car to pass, and eventually one did. I raised my arm and stuck out my thumb, but the car carried on. To be fair, would I have picked up such a hitchhiker on a remote coastal road in Nordland, Norway? I looked like someone in a horror movie, either the victim or the protagonist, or a student who had lost a day after a heavy metal concert. Dirty, once-white trousers, soggy trainers, no shirt, were all topped off by the wolf skin on my back, the only item of clothing I possessed that was truly warm. I had

72

no passport, money or identification. If the police found me, I would not be able to prove who I was, not least until I could make a phone call. I might well be in a great deal of trouble, especially if Morten came back and accused me of assault.

After an hour's walking I reached a bus stop, where I waited for half an hour. Nothing happened, except the sun was hanging in the sky and I grew weaker. When a very nice-looking Mercedes pulled up, I was hopeful. An old man got out and started speaking to me. He was local: I could tell because he spoke in the local dialect. It was a meeting of two cultures.

'Nar-vik? Trom-so?' I managed to say the words, but I could not have pronounced them correctly.

He stood there shaking his head at me, in his old trousers and checked shirt. I realised he was asking if I was all right. I smiled at him, stood up straight and showed him that I was fine. Then his face darkened and he spoke more harshly. He looked cross. He was telling me off! I took off the wolf skin, and revealed a bare chest, but that didn't help. He got back in his car and drove away.

If I'd had a pen and a large piece of cardboard, I could have written my destination in large letters and then everyone would have understood. I would have been transformed from potential threat to welcome traveller. But no-one else came along the road and I carried on, the coast behind me, heading to the point where route 80 forked east and west,

A white motor boat was sailing on the fjord with passengers on its deck, the black and white cross on red proclaiming the Norwegian flag fluttering behind it. I could have booked myself on such as boat as a paying customer. Instead, I had decided to take the cheap and difficult way of seeing the country.

The hopelessness of the situation began to hit me when I reached Løding. I was filthy and starving hungry. My throat was parched. A truck passed so close that I think the driver may have been trying to hit me, or to remind me that I was not wanted around here. I staggered on, my feet aching in my knackered shoes. When a minor road appeared on the right, I headed down it. At least there were some houses in sight.

CHAPTER 10

MAGNUS LOOKED IN the bathroom mirror to inspect his yellow eyes and yellowing skin. His guts hurt and rumbled. If he went to the doctor's they would ask questions, run their tests, and come up with nothing to help him, as usual. He ran a hand through his hair, and saw the natural darkness returning at its roots. Unlike most of the students at the university, Mette excepted, who were all naturally blonde, he relied on the magic genie in the bottle.

He blundered into the dormitory and took off his black coat and black shirt. He reached up to his bag, which was on the top bunk, and pulled from it a fresh T-shirt with a cool label, which he put on. Then he took the project tablet, which was charging from a small battery pack, and went to sit down at the end of the cabin. Everyone looked up, but he just dropped into a chair and ignored them with his earphones in, playing his music. He didn't say a word when the Professor came near and rather pointedly dropped his dilapidated boots by his feet. 'Deal with these please, Magnus. They stink.'

Magnus ignored him and swiped left and right on the tablet. No network! What was he to do for a week? Talk to the mosses! It was only when Mette brought him a bowl of noodles fortified with reconstituted dried fish, peas and beans that he took out his earphones and said thank you.

'We were lucky today,' she said, 'those boulders were enormous.'

He nodded. 'I know. I woke up in time to avoid being crushed. I felt like a mouse in a mousetrap.'

He didn't look at her, because he sensed she was looking at his skin. He put a hand to his face. 'This happens sometimes. No one can tell me why.'

Linnéa arrived and Mette moved along to the bathroom with her, where they closed the door. Jonas and Per were talking in low voices at the other end of the cabin, occasionally looking over at him. Magnus replaced his earphones and used the project tablet to listen to some nu-metal music. When Mette came out of the bathroom with Linnéa he was happily nodding along to the lyrics, at the same time playing a game which involved driving a car over the little creatures in his way.

The evening wore on and it bored him greatly. No internet connection meant there was no way of getting onto the forums where Magnus the Great was lauded. Certain people, ones whom he respected, knew about his earlier exploits on the mainland. His advice was being sought in coded messages, sent in a roundabout way, in case other people were looking or listening, but there was no way he could reply. It was very frustrating. Erik and the students played cards and told their idiot stories again. He shook his head when Mette asked him to play and asked whether there was anything wrong with the food.

Once the other students had eaten their dinner, he was satisfied the meal was not poisoned, so he ate up the cold bowl of fish, noodles and vegetables she had brought to him earlier. Soon there followed the familiar feeling of gas brewing in his guts, and a hot burning sensation under his ribs on the right side. His arms, legs and shoulders were all aching now. Those boulders had been big and tough but Magnus the Great had been bigger and tougher. He went to the bathroom and saw that his eyes were terribly yellow.

While the other students occupied themselves, he went into the dormitory and rummaged through their rucksacks and cases, which were standing on the floor. The Professor happened to come in for a book and almost caught him at it.

Linnéa and Mette had moved their wash bags from the bathroom so there was no more cotton wool to steal. He needed a new firestarter and he knew where to get it. Quietly, he opened the smoke detector at the end of the cabin and pilfered the nine-volt battery. He would need a length of wire as well, which he would look for later. He took his bowl to the kitchen and drew a sink full of water, as if he were washing up. But instead he slipped the ball of wire wool used to clean the pans into his pocket. He rinsed his bowl and left the other dirty bowls, glasses and cutlery untouched.

Magnus was the first to go to bed. He pretended to be asleep when the others came in later. He positioned the tablet under his blankets and took pictures of Mette as she undressed as she stood by her bunk. She was wearing what looked like a pink bikini under her work clothes. She knew what she was doing. Linnéa wisely changed in the bathroom. His clicking even managed to catch the Professor in his boxers when he thought everyone was asleep. Magnus chuckled but made it sound like he was snuffling and snoring. He couldn't wait to post these images on the forums!

In the morning Magnus woke with a feeling that his guts had brewed for him what he hoped to be his most deadly chemical attack to date. From his top bunk he laid an egg of such toxicity that Jonas and Per woke in dismay and stumbled out of the dormitory. The Professor slumbered on undisturbed, even though his bunk was directly below. Linnéa and Mette were furthest away and remained untroubled for a while.

Magnus was affected by his bombshell as well, and was weeping, not with disgust, but with laughter, when he entered the main cabin. He expected indignant complaints from Jonas and Per about the smell, but they each seemed to have grown a foot taller. They looked tired, with dark rimmed eyes as if they had not slept all night.

'Get your stuff, monster,' said Per. 'It's time for you to leave.'

Magnus stood in the middle of the room, towering over Per. 'You want to play, little man?'

Per brought out the project tablet and swiped his finger across the screen. There was Mette in her bikini, several shots as she undressed and changed into her nightclothes. Swipe: there was the Professor in his boxer shorts.

'Don't tell me you didn't enjoy at least one of those,' drawled Magnus the Great.

Swipe: a spinning red hammer appeared on the black screen. Magnus felt his guts go cold. He had deleted all mention of the forums, but somehow this website had remained in cache. He had visited it surreptitiously while they waited for their boat in Tromsø marina.

'Professor Nordveit would not like to see this from one of his students.' said Per. 'He is a liberal man, but he would say this crosses the line.'

'Actually, it would disgust him,' said Jonas. 'You know it is wrong. It is also illegal.'

Magnus looked down on Per, who was standing as if prepared for a fight.

'The game's up, monster,' said Per.

Jonas stood tall next to Per. 'As we all know.'

Magnus the Great recognised the look of men who would fight, but what hope did they think they had of winning?

Per moved past Magnus and unlocked the cabin door. The morning air was cold and fresh with sea spray. Jonas put a bag of food on the table: bread, apple, chocolate bar, a tin of fish, a stainless steel bottle of water.

'Take the food, and your sleeping bag. There is a cave on Trollveggen, which you may have found all ready.'

'Maybe I have, maybe I haven't.'

Jonas shrugged. 'Well done for making the fire. We saw the smoke yesterday, just before the boulders came down. You must have brought matches.'

Per showed him his lighter. 'This stays with me.'

Magnus grabbed for the lighter, but Per was too quick.

'If you go now then there will be no more trouble. We will tell the Professor that you wanted to be alone for the rest of the week.' Jonas held onto the tablet and the image of the spinning hammer. 'However, if you decide to stay, we will show the Professor this excrement, and he will call the police.'

Magnus bared his teeth. 'Idiot! Phones do not work here!'

'True,' said Jonas. 'But we have a satellite phone, locked away for emergencies. Didn't you read the field trip notes?' He smiled. 'It's your move, monster.'

His eyes flashed and his teeth gleamed as Magnus looked at the two young captains. They dare to command Magnus the Great, he thought. Are they dreaming? He looked again at the tablet's screen. He had been caught. The website was that of a banned organisation.

But so what? He did not fit in here with these pampered

students, with their silly stories and silly mosses. He grabbed the bag of food and set his face towards the open door. Per returned from the dormitory with his sleeping bag. He held it at arm's length and screwed up his nose. 'You will need this to keep warm.'

Magnus threw the bag of food and the sleeping bag into the enormous black sack he pulled out from his back pocket. As he walked past Jonas he imagined how the student's neck would feel in his hands, and how his back would break across Magnus's knee. Magnus breathed all over his face; Jonas recoiled in horror. Now Jonas was stunned he put some more items that had been placed near the doorway into his bag, knowing they would later curse him for having stolen them.

On his way out of the cabin Magnus grazed the side of his head on the door jamb and let out a howl. Then he stood on the deck and howled again. Outside he had friends in the air and in the sea. The cabin door was pulled shut quickly behind him and the key turned in the lock. The windows were closed up one by one.

Magnus the Great reached out and dragged the nails of his right hand like a claw over the metal university crest affixed to the cabin door. Five scars from his seemingly diamond-tipped talons were drawn through the two seabirds as his nails dug into the crest. The noise was beautiful to him; a chorus on five notes, an atonal shrieking as the birds died. The song marked out the occupants of the cabin for a similar fate. He tugged at the crest and left it hanging by one corner. The Professor would be cross with him, but would offer him a friendly chat, no doubt, with time and space to recant. Magnus spat on the hanging crest and watched his spittle drip to the ground.

The cabin door was unlocked and he heard soft footsteps

behind him. Mette stood on the deck, dressed in her white pyjamas. Her chocolate brown skin made her look delicious. 'Magnus,' she said quietly, 'say you're sorry. That's what people do when they make a mistake. We all make mistakes. Talk to the Professor, and say you're sorry. He will understand.'

Magnus stood on the deck outside the cabin. The wind was pure, the sky was bright, Trollveggen called to him. Why had he wasted so much time being cooped up inside with these fools?

'No, I choose my life out here,' said Magnus looking upwards. 'Sleep well,' he grinned, 'if you can.' He walked out over the survey area, kicking up clods of mosses, and looked about him to see what he needed to do next.

CHAPTER 11

T HE TREES LINING my route away from the highway only had a few tiny leaves. The sky was muddy brown in places. The light in these parts took the sky as its complete canvas. As I walked, the road widened out, until suddenly walls appeared on either side. On my left was a high wall with the tops of yet taller trees above it. On my right was a low wall, beyond which I could see a garden of forking paths and bushes. I kept to the middle of the road because the choice of left or right did not appeal, and perhaps because I wanted to keep my options open. Because of this, I almost missed the pale young woman who walked past me, close to the wall on my left. She was wearing a cloak with the cowl up, and had a wicker basket over her arm. I turned round and watched her as she reached the main road. She went along the way I had come and disappeared.

The pale-skinned woman of the north, walking away in the early fading light or twilight. The scene made quite an impression on me. But then I was tired, ill, hungry, thirsty and lost: precisely the circumstances that a mystic imagination would conjure up in order to open a door in either wall. I was wise to such old-fashioned ideas.

The largest of the houses was now on my left. This house was very grand: three floors high at least, maybe with attic rooms, with prominent botanical ornaments on the curved roofs. There were two stone steps leading up from the road to an iron gate hung between two man-high pillars. In the middle distance the sky was now streaked with yellow and orange. I resisted the idea that some intelligent force could be painting the sky.

Somehow, it felt warmer. I took off the wolf skin, which I was pleased to see had dried, and wrapped it around my arm.

'Keep the fur on,' said a man's voice. 'We all used to wear one.'

The voice came from behind the wall in the garden. I noticed a plume of white smoke rising.

'Come in, if you like, weary traveller. Take your rest.'

I walked up the steps, pushed at the gate, which was not locked, and entered the garden. A man of about sixty was bent down, crouching on his haunches. He was tying a bush of red roses to a vertical pole that ran up out of the ground to support it. A tall metal watering can stood nearby, its big thick spout pointing at me. The man continued with his work. He didn't look up as he spoke.

'Where are you going? Or perhaps you don't know the way.'

The man wore a light summer suit and a wide brimmed hat. The hat would have been perfect for beekeeping if it had had a veil attached although I didn't see any bees. He had a tanned leathery face and wore small round glasses. He seemed friendly and safe. For some reason, I thought he must be a school teacher.

The ground was the only place to sit. I arranged myself cross-legged on the dry, warm earth, some distance away from him so that I would not offend him with my smell. There was a grove of trees nearby, and a large wicker basket had been placed under one of them. The house had been white-washed

83

and had several large, shuttered windows. A tower room jutting out from the first floor was one of its distinctive features. The garden was neat, the many rows of tall roses, all supported by stakes, giving way to a white gravelled drive.

'This is a great country for travelling,' I said. 'Days merge into one another. You can really lose track of time.'

'Time!' The man laughed. 'Ah, yes, time.' When he smiled at me he looked very friendly. His leathery skin now made me think of the wise turtle from a popular children's film.

I considered this analogy. It was in the nature of walking, or questing (if this was what I was doing) that most encounters would turn out to be either neutral (the Norwegian man in the Mercedes who had stopped to berate me) or functional (the old lady in the church who had given me some beef broth). Occasionally encounters might become dangerous (let's say, Morten, but more likely the young lad in Bergen harbour). And very occasionally, this being the first example of one, an encounter might become numinous, especially when one's blood sugar level was low.

'It's a beautiful place,' I said, avoiding the topic of time. 'So much to see.' I knew I was being vapid and waited for the gardener to dispense his wisdom.

I must have been more tired than I thought, because the next moment I was looking up and he was looming over me. His legs and arms seemed as thick as the trees, and the brim of his hat was enormous.

'You carry no food, or water. Your satchel is empty.' My satchel was indeed in his hands. 'Your shoes are wet and ruined. Your clothes are thin, but the fur keeps you warm, for now.' He smiled down at me. 'And you stink like a farmyard animal.'

84

I struggled to my feet. 'I'm sorry to disturb you. I'll be on my way.'

He looked at me wide-eyed and close-lipped. Then a smile played across his face. 'Come and have a rest, tired traveller,' he said. 'My name is Bjarne.'

Here I was being helped by one of my tribe. There was no threat involved, no malice. He had just pointed out the obvious, that was all.

'That's very kind of you,' I said.

'Kindness!' he laughed, shaking his head.

He escorted me down the rose-lined path to a door into the house. The comfort of the place was palpable: there were soft chairs, rugs, and low lights. Some well-executed watercolours adorned the walls. 'These are good,' I said.

He inclined his head in a small Germanic bow.

I sat down on the wooden stool he offered me and took off my shoes. They were, indeed, wrecked. My feet were wet and swollen from walking. There were nasty red lines across the soles and blisters on the heels.

A warm yellow towel was placed in my hand. I dried my feet.

'You are on an adventure?' he said.

I nodded. 'Yes, I am. I am hitch-hiking across your country.'

'It used to be called journeying. We were all journeymen. On serious treks, we moved on foot while mules carried our tents.'

'Trekking, backpacking,' I said. 'It's still popular.'

He lit a cigar and offered me one a few inches long. The rolled leaves were the colour of dates or dark chocolate. I accepted the cigar and sniffed its wonderful earthy aroma. I even put it to my ear and heard a faint crackle when I rubbed it and felt the sponginess of the tobacco leaves.

He nipped off the tip of my cigar with a silver cutter and handed me a box of matches. The image of the flame, I knew, would stay with me a long time, because I had decided this was to be a numinous meeting. I was tired enough, and unsure of where I was going. I was at something of a crossroads. What would I learn, now that I had met a kindred spirit?

The cigar tasted good. I imagined fertile loam crumbling in my fingers, or my hand rubbing the bark of a tree.

He looked me up and down. 'You sail close to the wind, I think; living on your looks, and your wits. In other words, you survive by the skin of your teeth.'

I thought the cigar would be stimulatory, but I was falling asleep.

'I can do better than that for you.' He got up, and immediately his height and shape increased again. I struggled to stay awake. He pointed to a stone staircase leading down and out of the house. 'There is an area down there for washing.' He disappeared to some other room within the house to leave me alone.

I did as he suggested and found the stairway down to a bare stone-walled room that lacked a fourth wall; it opened out into the garden. The room was mostly filled by a large water butt with a pipe attached to guttering that collected rainwater from the roof. There was also a bucket and some soap. I was a dirty animal who would wash in rainwater and be ready to journey again the next day.

So I took off my stinking clothes and dropped them away from me. The spigot on the water butt was stiff, but eventually I managed to turn, and the water flowed into the bucket. I lifted the full bucket over my head, and then braced myself silently as the cascade of cold water hit me. The bucket slipped out of my hands and crashed on to the floor. I was simultaneously shocked by the cold of the water and the pain in my foot where the handle of the bucket had hit the knuckle of a toe. I was an animal, outside in the byre, washing itself down. I filled the bucket only halfway up next time and controlled better the icy sluice of water. When I had finished, I felt cleaner and refreshed. The cold water had temporarily quelled the riot in my guts, although I knew I was in for another episode before the day ended. I was also now very wide awake.

There was no towel, of course. So I stood in the early evening chill, and wiped the water off my body with my hands as best I could. Only in someone else's fantasy would I traipse through the house, naked, and ask for a large, soft towel. While I was drying myself, flicking the water off my arms and legs, I peered into the rest of the outhouse. There were hoes, rakes, spades, pitchforks and other tools hanging on the walls. The tools were well-kept. The spades were spotless; I found a thin layer of rust-denying oil when I ran my finger over a blade. There was also some hessian sacking, fit for a pilgrim, with which I gleefully rubbed myself dry.

When I returned to the wash room, there was a pile of clothes on the step: a blue tunic, beige trousers, thick white wool socks, and what looked like gym shorts. A pair of old brown shoes made up what I assumed to be a generous gift.

My own trousers were dispensable; I rolled them up and put them in the satchel. The wolf skin smelt very strong, like a dog in high summer. I filled the bucket with water again and dunked the fur in. The water quickly turned brown. I massaged and kneaded the fur. When I pulled the fur out of the water it had tripled in weight. I rolled, pressed and squeezed the water out of the fur, until it was just dripping steadily, no longer pouring.

I dressed in the new garb from the friendly gardener, smelling the freshness of the fabric as I did so.

When I went back upstairs Bjarne placed a bowl of meat stew in front of me on the table: diced meat, a grain like barley, potatoes and carrots.

'How do you like your new clothes?' he asked.

'There are very welcome, as is this food. I can't thank you enough.'

He frowned at me. 'Where is the wolf skin?'

'Downstairs, drying.'

He laughed. 'It will take days to dry in this weather.' He went downstairs and I heard him move through to the other room. I was halfway through my bowl of food when he came back. He handed me the wolf skin. 'It is still wet, so wear it open in the air, whatever anyone says.'

The fur was barely damp. 'How did you do that?'

'I have a press, a mangle.' He twisted his hands around an imaginary rope. 'It is the old way and the best.'

A memory of my great-grandmother's house rose up in front of my eyes. Near the back of the house, to the right of the door into the garden, where there were also rose bushes and chickens, was a room she used for laundry. There was a top loader and next to it a mighty piece of iron machinery. As a child I was warned, on pain of death, to keep well away from the turning wheels of the mangle.

Bjarne had settled back in his chair and was blowing a cloud of cigar smoke up to the ceiling. 'What is it that you like about our country?'

'There's a lot of space, but not many people.'

'You will find even fewer people on the roads. It is cheaper to fly or drive through Sweden.'

I wiped the stew from my chin. 'There are some nice expensive cars on the road, the usual German models mainly, and a few trucks. You never know who you're going to meet.'

'Where have you been, and where are you going; do you know?'

'I started in the south, in Bergen, and I intend to work my way up north.'

'The north? Why? There are even fewer people in the north!'

'I have no real idea. I just feel drawn there.'

'You did not have good shoes. You had no coat, just your fur. You have been lucky that we've had this heat wave. You have no tent. I guess you are camping, under bushes or trees?'

'I will do so if necessary. I have found shelter of a sort, in my own way.' The memory of the shack on the shore would never leave me, nor would dozing in Morten's car as the road flashed by.

'Why do you do it?' He asked. 'Are you looking for something?'

I had finished my bowl of stew and now I wanted to finish the cigar. He got up and re-lit it for me.

'I am not looking for anything specific, but if I do find something, and if it is right, then that's OK.' I thought for a moment about the book I had submitted for my art degree, about the self-analysis of its main character. 'It's very refreshing, at the moment, to be honest, just to be me.' I laughed at the pomposity of the statement.

'All this striving, all this reaching. Why don't you just give up?'

'Give up? Give up what?'

'Trying so hard. You will still be you.' He took a long pull on his cigar and blew a smoke ring.

I was taken aback.

'I suppose I could give up, but I don't know what the alternative is. There is no do, there is only try, as they say. If disaster strikes I have a number in my head to call and the back-up team of Mother and Father will swing into action.'

He puffed more smoke rings at the ceiling. 'No, that will not happen. You are not a mother's boy.' There was then a great silence between us, which was finally broken with a portentous question from Bjarne. 'Are you a wolf in the midst of sheep, or a sheep in the midst of wolves?'

If I had had a coin with me, I would have flipped it and let him know the result. Instead I said: 'That is a question that everyone must answer.'

We talked some more, until it had turned almost dark outside, with only a faint glow now showing from the sky. Bjarne offered me a place to sleep downstairs, which I accepted. In the middle of the night I was forced to rush to the bathroom to let the damage from the food poisoning course through me once again. However, I did feel my troubles were easing.

In the morning there were bread rolls, honey, and coffee for breakfast. Bjarne placed five twenty kroner notes on the table next to my plate. He waved away my protests. 'It is like looking at my younger self in the mirror,' he said. 'Keep safe, brave wolf.'

When I was ready to go Bjarne showed me to the front

door. We shook hands and he said goodbye, with a twinkle in his eye. I took the steps down to the road and was soon on my way into the dawn of the new day.

CHAPTER 12

E RIK HAD WOKEN up to find himself polluted by a terrible brown and green smell that had rolled down from the top bunk. For a moment he could hardly breathe. The dormitory was empty. He had to escape. He got up and rushed into the bathroom, where he was able to breathe again. He looked at himself in the mirror: dark rimmed eyes, pale face, with a grim line to his jaw. His grey hair stood up in a most unwelcome way. He opened the window and let in fresh air. There was a mist rolling down from Trollveggen. Magnus stood outside on a rock, looking at the cabin.

How much more of this, Erik groaned, and on my last field trip, as well?

When he entered the main cabin he saw Jonas and Per high-fiving. Both young men looked tired but happy. He noted the project tablet on the table: they must have been playing a game that had kept them up all night.

Per greeted him first. 'Good morning, Professor!' He reached over to the windows and drew open the curtains. The boulder field was deserted.

Linnéa appeared from the kitchen, gleefully clapping her hands. She then threw her arms around Jonas' neck and gave him a kiss on the cheek. Mette came in from the porch and looked sad, but at least the cold breeze had cleared away any remnants of the miasma left by Magnus.

Magnus' decision to leave the cabin in favour of Trollveggen did not surprise Erik very much. The other students explained over breakfast what had happened: Magnus had decided that enough was enough. He had tried to fit in, but he wasn't interested in the project. He just wanted to be alone.

'I agree that Magnus is a difficult person,' Erik conceded. 'As one counsellor explained to me, it is because he finds people so strange. They are peculiar to him, almost alien.'

'Anyway, it's all turned out for the best,' said Linnéa, slathering butter across her toast.

'I can see that this is a happy circumstance for some of us,' said Erik. 'Magnus is out of our hair for now. But he will have next to nothing to sustain him for the next few days. What does he have, exactly? A cold cave, a very limited supply of food and water, enough to last a day or two maybe? I wouldn't be surprised if he comes back tonight, tail between his legs.'

'Do you think Magnus does contrition?' asked Jonas.

Erik thought for a while. 'We will see. The question I need to consider is whether it is sensible to let Magnus risk his health on Trollveggen.'

Jonas protested. 'Professor, please, he is an adult! He can make up his own mind. People go backpacking with hardly any equipment all the time, sometimes not even a tent. They sleep in the bunkers on golf courses. They forage for food and water out of waste-bins. Magnus can make fire. He has a sleeping bag and I'm sure he's found the cave; that's why he was so keen to leave. He has Mette taking care of his breakfast, lunch and dinner, if he so wishes to take her charity. What more could a misanthrope want?'

'And Professor, with the greatest respect, you are not his father.' Linnéa was quite calm as she spoke. 'You are not *in loco parentis*. Magnus is an adult. He knows what he is doing, like pushing giant boulders down the mountainside to kill us.'

Mette was surprised. 'But he said it was an accident! He was caught out by the boulders falling as well.' She saw Jonas roll his eyes. 'Oh, I see.'

'Not everyone is as lovely as you, Mette.' said Jonas. 'Some people are twisted into a painful shape.'

'Well, there is little we can do about it,' said Erik. 'He is his own man.' While the argument for leaving Magnus outside seemed logical enough, what worried him was that others would find it irresponsible of Erik to leave Magnus to his own poor decisions. He told the students to get dressed for the day, as if he really was the parent in charge. Then he went to retrieve the SatPhone.

In the dormitory, Erik slid the metal locker out from under his bunk. He clasped the padlock in his hand and turned the four wheels on the combination lock. He expected the padlock to open when he pulled the clasp, but it remained closed. He frowned, spinning the wheels of the combination and lined up the same numbers, with the same result. He dialled in another combination, and another. He looked at the padlock for a few moments, willing it to open. This cannot be happening to me, he thought. Erik only used two four-digit number combinations, which he remembered from his bank cards. He tried them both again, again with no result. The locker was impregnable; any bashing it would bring them running into his embarrassment. He slid the locker back under his bed.

'Are we all ready?' Erik asked, when he returned to the cabin.

'Looking forward to it, Professor,' said Jonas. 'We've worked hard to get on this research trip ... well, most of us have.' Jonas poked Per in the ribs.

'I've worked hard,' said Linnéa. 'So has Mette. And we're not sorry that Magnus has decided to leave.'

'He's still out there,' said Erik. 'And once he comes to his senses, he will realise that living outside in these conditions is a romantic dream.'

'I don't see Magnus as a romantic dreamer,' murmured Jonas.

'Indeed, no,' said Erik. He took a deep breath. 'If you do see Magnus, however, please let me know immediately, and I will go and talk to him.'

Erik pushed open the door of the cabin. He looked around and checked that Magnus wasn't hiding on the porch. Jonas and Per emerged next, followed by Linnéa and Mette. Per had been keen on this defensive formation and had wanted to go first. To protect the women and the potential children, thought Erik, although he might still be too young to see it in that way. Protect the human race from the monsters, thought Erik, wasn't that more like it? So Erik was first out on to the deck. He reasoned from an old-fashioned sense of authority that Magnus was least likely to attack a Professor. Magnus was a difficult case, but he was still human.

Then Erik saw the mess Magnus had made of the university sign and part of him died. He took down the sign and cradled it in his chair on the deck, as if the sea birds really had been killed by a long-clawed monster. He might not be able to remember the combination to the locker, and therefore the SatPhone was unavailable to him, but there was still the radio in the boat. He would call his colleagues now and ask them what to do about the problem that was Magnus.

As he approached the jetty he heard a familiar flapping sound and saw that the edge of the tarpaulin at the back of the boat was undone again. A single gust of wind lifted the loose flap and folded the tarpaulin over, making the inside of the boat ready to inspect. He could not believe that his knots had come undone again.

All appeared fine until he saw that the outboard motors were sitting too low in the water. He had pulled them up with Per when they secured the boat after landing. He ran his hand around the engine casing. There was a hole where a panel had been taken off and the starter motors removed. His mouth went dry, his saliva sticking to his teeth. This was unheard of; Magnus had been deliberately sabotaging university property and endangering them all. He looked up at Trollveggen. Magnus must be up there laughing as he watched the Professor inspect the damage.

Erik boarded the boat and checked the wheelhouse. There was nothing obviously wrong until he found that the fuse panel had been pulled out from under the dashboard and all the fuses were missing. He took the boat key out of his pocket and thrust it into the console, turning it. No lights flickered on the instrument panel. He checked again and saw that the twelve-volt battery was also missing. Carried up the mountain, or dumped into the sea? Either way, the boat had no power. He picked up the radio and saw that it was dead. This thorn in his side called Magnus had disabled his favourite boat.

He tied up the tarpaulin once more. Do not let your anxieties affect the students, he reminded himself. You are in charge and everything will be fine.

The students worked well once they were all convinced that Magnus really had gone up Trollveggen and was staying there. At midday Erik inspected their work. Jonas and Linnéa had done a thorough job of recording the species they had sampled on the line transect. The samples had been taken every five metres, as instructed. The knees of their trousers were wet and muddy, the badge of honour of kneeling down and taking notes. They deposited their samples in the freezer in the basement of the cabin.

'Do you think this extended survey will really make an impact?' Jonas asked. 'What if we found pollutants all over the island; what would we do?'

'We would alert the monitoring network, and then the environmental ministry. The situation could easily become political if the source of the pollution was trans-boundary. Our country would protest in the strongest terms.'

Linnéa stood up from where she was working and shook back her hair. 'So we will have impact, impact, impact,' she said, clapping her hands together as Erik liked to do in lectures.

'Yes, quite possibly. In fact it is a win-win-win situation.' He clapped his hands together three times in response. 'If the levels of heavy metals are still high, then we need to know about it. Alternatively, if the levels have subsided, everyone will be pleased about that, too. Whatever happens, we will have shown people the value of what we do here on Svindel. People value their health, of course, especially from unseen threats.'

He looked towards Trollveggen. Walking up over the boulder field would have been difficult, even for Magnus. The rocks were slippery from some light rain; from previous trips Erik remembered how he would always be the one to find the loose stones. His feet hurt in his house shoes as he walked up the slope. Per had lost his bright yellow sea boots and was wearing Erik's boots instead.

Erik stepped out into the foothills. Trollveggen was one wall of a volcanic crater that had risen abruptly out of the sea: it was an improbable but real reminder of how things came to be. He stepped carefully between the boulders, half expecting to find Magnus asleep behind one of them, or, maybe even more likely, waiting to jump out at the Professor.

As the climb became harder, Erik bent forward to grab handholds in the earth and rocks. Then the slope quickly got too steep and he had to stop. He would need to get his hiking boots back from Per if he was to make the trip up to Bø's cave. No doubt Magnus was already there.

Then he saw the white poles and red flags, discarded in the middle of a group of rocks. Plastic sample bags fluttered in the breeze. He caught them all up and stuffed them in his coat pockets. Magnus had dumped all of his project kit here. He had done no work at all: not even planted one flag. There was no sign of him. Erik's blood boiled. He had tried, he really had tried very hard indeed. Magnus had been given every chance, but he had failed to grasp any of them. He was now showing his true colours; sloth, indolence, violence to property. It was clear he didn't care about authority.

He scrambled back from the foothills, passing Jonas and Linnéa. 'Lunchtime in half an hour,' he said. The day was warming up again and the sky was a pleasant light grey. They would have lunch outside on the deck. 'I'll go and get Per.'

When they gathered for lunch, Jonas acted as lookout and then Per took over. 'We will do the same tonight,' said Per, 'as we did last night.'

'I will join you in your plan,' said Erik. He put away the wrecked sign from the cabin door and tried to remember the four-digit combination he needed.

CHAPTER 13

MAGNUS THE GREAT climbed up Trollveggen at a crawl. Every time he looked back, he saw the pastoral idyll of the golden cabin on a field of green, lit up by a light grey sky and surrounded by a glistening blue sea. Erik and the students were now on the deck eating lunch. He willed one of the boulders downhill again and in his fantasy it did not fall short this time, but crushed them all to death while they talked about how good life was without him.

He was in pain; panting heavily, back and legs aching; his right side, under his ribs, felt as if it was on fire. At the spot where he had dumped the contents of the bag on his first ascent, he now picked up a few flags and plastic bags. The cave was bare: these might be useful. He had opened his sack and tried on Per's yellow sea-boots, but they were far too small. It had been a real shame: the steel toe caps, and rubber soles would have helped him over the slippery slopes and boulders. Both of the yellow search-and-rescue sea boots flew into the sea; they floated for a while before disappearing out of sight.

He carried on toiling upwards, trying to ignore the pain. Another hour's slow scrambling took him to the huge rock and boulder field below the summit. He found the chimney at the top of the cave again and dropped the sack down it. The black leather split open as it hit the ground and out tumbled bread rolls, bananas, several small tins, and a cabbage that rolled a few feet and stopped dead like a head. A metal water bottle lay like a bomb waiting to explode. The sleeping bag spilled out and lay invitingly on the floor.

He sat down at the lip of the chimney, poked his legs into the opening, and secured footholds for his boots in the rock on each side. Then he lowered himself down through the chimney until his head was inside the cave and his back was against the solid rock. Going down was more difficult than going up. He moved too fast initially and grazed the back of this head on the wall. His howling reverberated around the cave. He liked the sound and yelled again. All of the birds on the cliff edge took off over the sea. Magnus the Great was back.

He slipped down the last couple of metres and jumped on to the cave floor, where he trod on a banana, the white flesh oozing over the ground. He was exhausted. He lay down and rested, lying on his back. He slept for a while, until his heart had calmed down.

When he woke up, a voice was calling to him. The voice of a woman. He looked up and hoped to see Mette, although he questioned how it could possibly have been her; she would be in the cabin with his enemies. It was the voice of an older woman, his mother.

Magnus the Great looked up at the opening to the cave and knew exactly where he was and why he was here. He got up and walked to the cave entrance and looked out over the north of the island, where the sea crashed into perpendicular cliffs. He scanned the area to the right of the cave entrance, where there was a steep slope heading down to the south-western side of the island; it was approachable at a cost, but only if that route was not being watched.

The midnight sun was sitting on the horizon, lighting up

his new home. He picked up some of the flags the Professor had given him and stuck one in the ground at the back of the cave. He took off his grey T-shirt with the black patches under the arms. He placed another flag across the first vertical flag and set it about two thirds of the way up. He would need rope or string to bind the flags together, but for now he would use the belt from his designer denim jeans. The jeans slipped down his legs and he stepped out of them. He dressed the tailor's dummy with the grey T-shirt. His mother could look good in anything. He apologised to her because the cabbage was all that he had for a head. He pulled the red pennant off the flag that was his mother's spine and poked the green cabbage on top. Another red flag transformed itself into a headscarf for his mother. Red was her favourite colour.

Finally, he had a companion in his new home. A roaring fire was his next job. He used up the last of the cotton wool balls soaked in petroleum jelly and the last of the bird's nest. He soon had a fine fire going; he warmed his hands then entire body in the flames. He made shadows on the wall by dancing around. Really, it was the most fun he had ever had in his life.

He smiled as an idea took shape. With a chalky stone he marked four lines on a dark grey patch on the wall of the cave. Four days to Midsummer's Eve, and then there would be a reckoning! He tore chunks out of a bread roll with his teeth, and relaxed as he sat behind the fire looking out over the sea and dipped the bread into a tin of sardines.

His mother spoke for the first time, confirming his thoughts as if she was psychic. The golden cabin which housed the Professor and four students was indeed strong and well supplied, but her son knew its layout and the personalities of his enemies. The boat was tied up at the jetty and bobbed prettily on the tide, but it was no more use to them unless they wanted to risk being dragged out to sea and sucked into the whirlpool.

Maybe the Professor really did have a satellite phone and could call down an air strike on their heads or fill the island with Politi and counsellors. He was taking his time if that was true. In any event, Mette would speak up for Magnus and say that he didn't really present a threat. He imagined her sitting next him by the fire and it was a lovely thought.

Next morning, he climbed up out of the chimney and started to figure out the best route up and down the mountain. He stood amongst the boulders near the summit, out of sight of everything except the birds, sun and sky. The morning sunlight lit up the golden roof of the cabin; it was a truly beautiful sight. What had the students and their Professor been up to? He would have to take a look.

He tried out a new route to the cabin, employing a flanking manoeuvre rather than a frontal assault. There was just room to walk on the ledge that ran across the top of the cave entrance; he knew that if he slipped he would simply fall into the sea, just like those boulders which had smashed on the rocks. The wind buffeted his tall frame, making him cautious. Lying on his belly, he slithered along, hidden behind the huge rock that marked the summit of Trollveggen. When he got to the very top he followed the rock around to the right and, apart from the need to dodge a few boulders, the going was now much easier. The wind was at his back. If he had extended his arms he would have been able to fly.

The northern slope down the mountain was steep but accessible. His boots sank into softer ground and he could feel the earth between his toes. He was able to move more quickly by slipping down on his backside. He traversed a flat rocky plateau littered with dark boulders. On the seaward side it was easier to walk down the slope, from which he could see the copse of trees ahead. There were a few large rocks to step over and pick through, but nothing impeded Magnus the Great. The weather tower came into view. He would play on it for a while, as if it were a climbing frame in a playground.

Wending through the copse of trees, walking on silent rock, with no warning stones scattered in front of him, he was essentially invisible to those in the cabin. Unless they had posted Jonas and Per as lookouts - but what a dull job that would have been. And were they really brave enough to stand outside the golden cabin and look out for someone they called the "monster"? Exiled, estranged, outsider, even refugee: he had heard all these words before from many well-meaning but ultimately stupid people who just didn't understand what it was like to be someone who hated nearly everyone.

The websites and forums were illegal: that was true, and, he had to admit, with good reason, because there were others like him at large in the world. If the police should arrive, they would question Magnus and he would have to refuse to tell them who had given him access to the websites. He would be a marked man. The university might not give him his stupid degree. Magnus the Great would end up with very little at all. So he would have to fight back.

He stopped at the edge of the copse of trees. There was a clear path across the carpet of mosses; it led to the weather tower. The wind had gotten up and was bringing in the spray off the white-tipped waves. There were no sentries; everyone was hidden safely away inside the cabin. There were no windows at the far end of the dormitory, so no one would see him coming. He walked over to the tower, put one hand on the cold metal and began to climb. Every few seconds he waited and listened. He could hear no sound coming from the cabin. The windows were probably tightly fastened. He could see the faint golden glow of lights from behind the curtains and the occasional moving shadow.

Magnus loitered on the tower and waited. A satellite phone, was that really true? Then why hadn't the police arrived already? He looked towards the jetty. The project motor yacht glistened white; there were no other boats. There was no sound of a helicopter overhead as the cavalry arrived.

Magnus climbed up the tower to the highest point he dared go, to within touching distance of the spinning silver cups that directed air to the sensors. He felt his body weight being drawn back to earth, even though the wind was light. Seven-foot, eighteen stone, he was a great man. His hand grabbed the first metal cup and tore it free. It floated up in the air and then plummeted gently to the ground. The three remaining cups continued to spin in the breeze, driving the air in to a metal box, which he tugged at but could not dislodge: it was securely fixed. One by one, he plucked the silver cups from their stems, like flower heads from a rose bush, or like students on a field trip. To be great was to be merciful. Would he spare anyone? He decided that he would spare Mette, who was the sweetest dish.

All four cups floated downwind and landed softly on the moss carpet. Sadly, yes, mother; you heard the news correctly. Four people fell asleep in the dormitory never to awake. Carbon monoxide poisoning; the generator had been faulty. Only two students had survived. One student had been leaving food outside for another student who, for some reason, had been camping out in a cave on his own. Questions were asked about how the Professor in charge of the field trip could have allowed such a thing to happen. It turned out that the student who was camping had been evicted from the cabin owing to an outrageous case of malicious peer pressure. The young woman who had been leaving the food out for the unfortunate man appeared to be the only one who had taken pity on him.

Magnus smiled; the cold air tasted so good on his teeth. He and Mette would decide to stay on the island a while, maybe for a few days or several weeks; friends would bring in their supplies.

His foot slipped on the metal rung and for a moment he felt himself falling. He was interested by the sensation of weightlessness, but also by his own response. He grabbed the tower with his free hand and replanted his boot on the rung. Magnus the Great was truly a survivor and destined for great things. He was not a skydiver without a parachute, a cliff climber destined to fall; he was truly the King of the Mountain!

His eyes now fell on Trollveggen, at the end of the island. It was the legacy of a volcanic eruption formed by outpourings of fire. He likened it to the acid from his stomach that plagued him constantly; it was a fitting home for him. He wondered if he might be related to a fire-breathing dragon. He jumped down the last metre of the tower; it proved to be a mistake. The pain that pierced his side would have vented itself as a wolf's howl if he had let it. There was the pain again, now, below his right kidney, in the vicinity of his liver.

The cabin door opened. The lovely Mette came out. She walked on the path through the survey area to the boulder field and placed a white bag on the nearest boulder. When she turned around to return, Magnus stood behind the tower and kept very still. He was pleased that he had chosen so well the woman to carry on his line: how he would like to place Mette in his sack and carry her away with him right now. But he was confused by how a dark woman could be kind to a white man when his own kind hated him so much.

Mette returned to the cabin and locked the door. All was quiet. Magnus the Great thought of some excellent entertainment for his fans. He stepped silently on to the deck, undid his fly, and pissed against the cabin door. The dark urine ran slowly down the frame, seeping into the gaps in the wood.

He moved away quickly now, struggling not to laugh. He discovered he could command stealth, despite his large frame; this would allow him to move about the island unopposed at night. It was a wonderful feeling. He loped back up the mountain to his cave, to think some more.

CHAPTER 14

THE SUN CAST a light glow over the road as I headed away from Bjarne's house. I had thought about his question and decided that I was indeed a wolf in the midst of sheep. I placed the head of the pelt on top of my own head; there was no-one around for me to annoy or dismay, and for a while I liked the idea of looking like a wolf. I certainly wasn't about to give up my quest: for one thing, Mother and Father would not be impressed.

I reached the junction near Løding again and took the route that would eventually lead me to Narvik. I walked along the side of the wood, keeping the wolf head hanging off my shoulders, not wanting to put off anyone from giving me a lift. At around eight o'clock - I guessed the time, having been without a watch so long that I'd got quite good at it - several cars passed by me heading to and from Bodø and the ferry terminal. I hung out my thumb in the hitch-hiker's universal gesture of hope, but no-one stopped or even slowed.

I carried on up the road, feeling on top of the world. It's amazing what a bit of glucose in the blood stream does to a person. I would need revitalising again later, however, so I stopped at a service station. I found some food in a dumpster behind the car wash: a plastic case of mini pastries covered in icing. The pastries had been squashed and doused with some sort of fruit juice. I selected the two best-looking ones and saved them for later.

Five minutes later, a car passed me and stopped up ahead, its lights flashing. The woman driver pushed open the door of the BMW and called to me to get in.

'Thanks,' I said. 'Takk.'

'Having a wander, are we?'

'I was at a concert last night,' I grinned. 'Not sure how I got here.'

'It must have been a good concert. Who was it?'

We glanced at each other in the rear-view mirror.

'Metal Death, on one of the islands.'

She didn't look back again. 'Each to their own,' she said. 'I'm heading a little way north, past Narvik, and then I'll cross the border to Sweden at Riksgränsen. Where are you headed?'

'Narvik or Tromsø. It doesn't matter. I'm just seeing the sights.'

'There's much more to see in Tromsø. They call it the Paris of the North.' She checked the mobile phone plugged into her dashboard. 'There is a problem with the road north to Tromsø: a land slip has closed both lanes. Such a shame, it's normally a lovely drive all the way north to Kåfjord on the E6. It's called the Arctic Highway, you know, it goes through the mountains.'

She thought for a moment. 'If you can get to Harstad there's a ferry that will take you in to Tromsø.'

I checked that I had the hundred kroner in the pocket of my new trousers. 'I'll do that.' For the first time in a few days I had a plan of action. I reached out my hand. 'Alexander.'

She squeezed my hand. 'Ramona.'

The back seat was full of cases of paper cups, packets of napkins, bags of plastic cutlery.

She saw me looking. 'I work in catering.'

We spent the next five hours on the road, cars blurring past on the left, my new friend driving expertly along on the right. The sky was blue and studded with a few cotton wool clouds. I didn't discuss the weather; how incongruous would that have been from the wolf in the back. The road became long and fast and we zipped along. As we alternated between the coast and travelling inland to the opposite side of the country, the sea appeared on the right and then, with the change in the route, on the left. Ramona dipped the lights as we drove into tunnels and then we re-emerged into the sun-shine. She was happy to give me a lift all the way to a village called Berjvik, where I would take a bus to Harstad, and she would head for Sweden. And for that kindness, I pilfered a blue biro from the hollow in the door handle.

We stopped to have a rest break in Narvik, and then took the ferry over the fjord. Ours was the first car allowed on and we were able to park right at the front of the ship. The ferry sailed across the sea and delivered us to the next section of road to Berjvik. When we arrived, Ramona got out of the car and stretched her legs. We looked over at the fjord together.

'My favourite place,' she said. 'The light at this time of year is incredible.' The summer heatwave was working its magic, lighting up the snow-capped hills and warming the sea. 'Are your friends still on Lofoten?'

'Yeah. Wait till the guys hear about this.'

We found the bus stop I needed and inspected the time-table to Harstad. There was a bus at six-thirty that evening.

'I'm sorry it departs so late.' Ramona looked worried. 'There's not much to do around here.'

'You've done enough already.' There was a sign with an arrow that pointed down to the rocks at the water's edge. I went first, and she followed me, down to a wide beach on the edge of the fjord. We bared our feet and dipped them in the freezing cold water. Ramona seemed captivated by the sea; I guessed that she'd decided that her business in Sweden could wait. Then our eyes met and her interest in me became more pronounced. She stripped off her clothes and ran into the sea; she didn't even flinch at the cold. I guessed that was the sort of fun they liked around here, so I did the same, dumping the new clothes given to me by Bjarne on the beach. The shock of the sea was exhilarating, like the cork coming out of a champagne bottle.

We splashed one another and swam a few yards out and then back again, mindful of the strong current trying to pull us away from the shore. I showed off my ability to turn handstands in the water. When I surfaced for the third time, Ramona was sitting, naked, on a rock on the shore waiting for me. She had one hand on her chest, and her long golden hair was around her neck and shoulders.

She looked beautiful and I felt desire thrill inside me. I walked out of the sea back up the beach to her, penis and balls shrivelled to walnuts. We lay down on her clothes behind a rock and I recovered rapidly from the cold. Later I supposed the wolf skin had played its part, turning me into a character that may have excited her since childhood.

We dressed and hugged each other goodbye. She drove away, giving me a last wave as she steered her BMW back on the road to Sweden. This was what I had hoped for from my long summer away; it was picking up splendidly, or so I thought, but briefly. A nagging thought struck me; I checked my pockets. The five twenty kroner notes were gone. I opened my satchel and saw that Ramona had even taken the pastries. I wished her well with that windfall, given their providence. So, I had been taken for a ride, literally and metaphorically; yet it was still better to be a wolf than a sheep, dear Bjarne. Given the commerce between myself and Ramona, it was difficult to bear a grudge.

I dressed and waited for the bus while wondering what I would do in Tromsø. Perhaps I could teach English to students as a foreign language? Of course I had no qualification, or even a passport, and legally I wouldn't be allowed to stay here much longer, but apart from those troublesome details, I believed it to be a possibility. Or perhaps I could teach English and Maths, if my pupils weren't really clever kids: no point in getting shown up by the students. I didn't think I could teach Art; I don't think it can be done.

Two young men came running up the beach and dived into the water. They each wore dark blue beach shorts, as if they were part of a team, and I immediately wanted a pair for myself. One of the young men came over to me. He was laughing. He mimed the coupling of a man and a woman. I affected nonchalance.

'English?' he asked? He squinted at me, because the sun was shining over my shoulder.

I thought about being French, or German, or a deaf mute, but that was no way for a wolf to behave.

'Yes, English. I'm travelling to Harstad.'

'Ah,' he said, as if that explained everything. 'Go and see Sigrid. She likes the travellers.'

'Sigrid? What does she do?' It seemed obvious to me what I was hinting at, but apparently this was not what the young man had in mind.

'She needs interesting people to do work for her.'

'OK. Where do I find her?'

The young man pointed down the beach at a blue and white quay, at the end of which a white boat bobbed up and down on the lapping waves. 'Ask those men, they will tell you.'

'Go and see Sigrid,' he repeated and so I decided I would. If it didn't work out I could catch the next bus, which was due in four hours.

I headed for the boat at the quay and something about that short walk down the beach filled me with cheerfulness. I had shed one skin and was growing another, while moving on to the next leg of my journey.

There was a man who looked like a chef cooking on a black iron grill next to the quay. The aroma of fish was greeted by a happy rumble from my stomach and I knew that my guts were on the mend. When I got up close I saw rows of silver fish, glistening like the waves. When the man turned the fish over, the silver skin was charred across with black lines, which made them yet more tempting. He tossed some fish on to hunks of white bread, then squeezed lemon on the burnt flesh; I had to look away as I imagined the taste. The man's customers handed over coins and walked away with their food, going to sit on the rocks and contemplate the sea.

If I had only one silver scale of the many that had adorned my cloak, I would have freely given it to pay for a fish sandwich, but I had nothing. I wore a wolf skin and no doubt looked like a charity case. So I hung back and watched two young men offloading cargo from the boat that stood bobbing on the waves. The one on the boat was passing boxes to the one on the quay.

The chef cooked his fish for the people who ebbed and flowed up and down the beach. The sky was mauve and dimly lit at the horizon by the sun struggling through the clouds. The view would suit painters who liked stormy and unsettled scenes: those looking for a clear aspect and an insight into nature's true reflection would not find it here.

And then we all heard a splash. I looked over at the boat and saw a turtle drop out of the bottom of a cardboard box and dive into the sea. The two men swore as they stood looking over the edge of the boat, then under the quay for the turtle. The sound of young men swearing at one another is the same in any language, even though there was some Norwegian detail. They were blaming each other and looking at the soggy hole in the large box from where the turtle had escaped. The man on the quay jumped into the water and dived down as deep as he could go. He soon came up again, shouting abuse at his companion. I could have told him how cold the water was.

I walked over to the boat to take a better look. One of the men saw me approach and put out his hand to stop me in my tracks. I did as he meant me to. His friend and he looked at me warily as they stood discussing the situation on the boat. Then the first man hopped on to the quay, suddenly full of smiles.

'Hello,' he said in Norwegian.

'Hei,' I responded.

'Tourist?' he tried in English.

'Traveller' I nodded, pointing to his boat. 'I go to Sigrid.' Then my stomach rumbled, and I rubbed it. 'Please, I am hungry.'

CHAPTER 15

Erik looked up from the dining table when Mette came in from outside.

'So you have been the Good Samaritan again?' he said.

'It is my food which I am giving him, Professor. I cannot bear the idea of him suffering out there.'

'It was his own choice, Mette. I agree with the others now. Magnus is an adult.'

Mette shook her head. 'What's so great about being an adult? It's just a number. Some people reach their twenties and thirties still having the mind of a child.'

'Magnus has been declared mentally competent by any number of experts.' Erik gestured to her to sit down, but she declined. 'He has some food and water now. He has his sleeping bag. Jonas and Per tell me he has found the cave.'

She looked towards the cabin door as if she heard something. 'I hope that cave keeps him nice and warm. Magnus wants to be a real Nordlending!'

'That's half his problem. He wants to be the boss in a situation where he needs to follow the rules.' Erik smiled. 'I had thought he was trying. He even dyed his hair blonde to try and blend in.'

'He's a guy trying to look his best. It's normal.' She moved on to join the other students, who were playing cards.

Erik dug out another paper from his briefcase and sat back in his favourite chair to read it. His heart sank when he realised the report contained some mathematical modelling. Even a trip to the fridge for a cold beer didn't help quell the tension it caused in his head. He skipped reading most of the paper and relied on the abstract and the discussion published with it instead.

He had been reading the same paragraph over and over when Mette and Linnéa said goodnight. They were shortly followed by Per and Jonas, who having finished their beers and cards were ready to turn in. Erik selected another paper to read, enjoying the peace in the empty room. At one point he looked up at the front door of the cabin, thinking perhaps he could smell something strange. He soon settled down again and carried on reading until one o'clock, when he walked back to the dormitory. He welcomed the fresh smell and the walls of green as he changed and pulled the thick blanket over him.

Erik slept like a log and then switched on like a light in the morning. He was the first awake. He got up, dressed, and looked around the dormitory. Linnéa's white gold hair was piled into a bun on her pillow. Jonas was sleeping half in, half out of his bag, his long legs draped over the side of the bunk and resting on the floor. A third, much larger sleeping bag had been made from two; it breathed with a life of its own and inside Erik could hear whispering. He tiptoed past.

In the main cabin all seemed well. He drew back the curtain and looked out of the window. The sky was light grey, the sea choppy. No obvious change had taken place outside the cabin. The front door was locked; Erik tugged the handle gently. But there was a bad smell in the entrance area that he couldn't place. He wondered if some food was going off in the kitchen or basement.

Going down to the basement himself, he brought up more breakfast supplies. They still had plenty of long-life milk and crispbread. Supplies of fruit and vegetables were holding up; and if they ran out, they could survive for weeks on tinned food, although they were low on chocolate and snacks. Their water supply was fine.

Jonas came in and sat down at the table. He was dressed only his boxer shorts and T-shirt. He moved the beer bottles and crisp packets to one side and lay down his head on the table.

'Good morning, Jonas. Did you not sleep well?'

'It was noisy.' He raised his head. 'Never mind.'

'How about a drink. Tea, coffee, or spiced honey?'

'Ah, the drink of royalty, how expensive that would have been in the past.'

'I'm sure I can spare some if you like it.'

'No, thank you, just hot water for me.'

Erik grinned. 'My wife drank only hot water throughout her pregnancy.'

Per appeared. 'That's your feminine side coming out, Jonas.'

'And where's your feminine side, or is she still asleep?'

Per grinned from ear to ear but said nothing. He accepted the offer of a cup of coffee from Erik.

'I've been thinking about Magnus,' said Erik. 'What are we to do? We cannot let him stay outside again for another night. He will freeze to death, if he isn't a corpse already.'

Jonas clicked his fingers, as he did when he had an idea. 'That's easy. We clear out all the supplies from the basement and keep them up here. Then we tell Magnus that he can live in the basement until Monday, when we all go home.' Jonas rested his head on the table again.

'That's not very helpful,' said Erik.

'Funny, though,' said Per, 'it would be like keeping a pet monster.'

'Mette left him a parcel of food and water last night,' said Erik.

'He's a strong guy,' said Per, 'he chose his new way of life; he can get on with it.'

Jonas raised his head again. 'Professor, any luck with the combination?'

The question was a surprise and a jolt. So they knew he was struggling. He felt fallible. He felt himself blushing, so he turned away.

'Not yet, but I will remember it soon, I'm sure it will come to me just when we need it the most. Sometimes memory cannot be forced.'

'That's true,' said Per. 'I can't remember anything in the exams.'

'It's because you never learnt it in the first place: at least not in a form you could recall. And that's a trick that needs lots of practice, but who practises their knowledge in the many months and weeks before an exam? You have to do a little bit, often, that's the only trick there is.'

'We should be told this in the first year.'

'You are told this in the first year, but it doesn't sink in.'

'But if you don't remember the combination, Professor, then we have to wait until the next project group gets here. The radio on the boat is disabled. Our mobile phones do not work. Magnus has done quite a job on us. How's the food situation?'

'Good. We have lots of water as well. That is one commodity we do have. Although I would like to ask you to go fishing, if you don't mind.'

Per's eyes sparkled liked the break of a shoal of fish on the sea. 'It takes time and skill to catch fish with only a rod and line. I would need to be excused my project work.'

'We need to eat fresh food and keep our morale up, so I have to let you do it,' said Erik. 'Although my colleagues will not be at all impressed if I waive your project requirements.'

'Your colleagues didn't come on a field trip where they needed to contend with a proper live troll.'

Jonas and Per laughed together.

'Don't call him a troll,' said Mette, entering the room. 'He's a person.'

'Sorry,' said Per.

Mette looked almost too good to be true. Her hair was washed, her skin glowed; she seemed energised. Erik had never seen her so alive.

'Good morning, Professor,' she said.

'Good morning, Mette.'

Linnéa eventually appeared after breakfast, and although she said hello, she was quiet as she ate a piece of unbuttered toast and drank some tea. The students discussed their project work with Erik, including Per in the conversation even though he had now been officially tasked with spending his time fishing. The Anti-Magnus Plan was discussed, although Mette renamed it the Magnus Contingency. They were to present to Magnus as a group if he came calling and keep in mind the idea of safety in numbers. They would make it clear that they could offer him food and water.

'What if he wants to come back in?' asked Mette.

'He won't,' said Per.

'Yeah, but what if he says he wants to, you know, just in order to test us?' asked Jonas.

'I will tell him that he is not allowed to make any further use of university property. He has caused enough damage already: the boat, the sign on the cabin door, the personal items that have gone missing. He has given us many reasons to exclude him from this part of the campus.'

'Can you do that?'

'This situation is unprecedented. I can only act from my initiative.' Erik sighed. 'This will be my last field trip. If there are any ramifications, or I am asked to resign, then I will be forced to retire anyway. I will make it easy for my superiors to close the case.'

'So this is your kingdom and you will defend it from a terrible monster.'

'As best I can, with what I have. Although, if a hero was to turn up, someone who had the equal might and cunning of Magnus, that would make a good story as well.'

'We can give Magnus some blankets, to go with his sleeping bag,' said Linnéa.

'That's a good idea,' said Jonas. 'We can also give him the tarpaulin from the boat. It is impermeable to the weather.'

'The tarpaulin weighs a ton,' said Per. 'He'll never get it up to the cave.'

'He's not a dog to be kept outside!' exclaimed Mette. 'Perhaps he could sleep in here, or in the basement.'

Linnéa was not happy. 'There is no way on earth that that freak is sleeping in the cabin again, no way. I could barely sleep the first night when he was here. He hates us, he absolutely hates us. However sorry you feel for him, Mette, he's got major problems, and those problems threaten our safety.' She lowered her voice, as if Magnus was listening. 'You know people say he killed his girlfriend?'

'It was never proved,' said Erik. 'The cause of death was given as accidental drowning.'

'And the girlfriend's brother died accidentally at the same time, too! Now that's a coincidence you would reject in any research data, Professor.' Linnéa was pale with the exertion of her argument.

'I agree it doesn't look good for Magnus,' said Erik.

'Then why did you let him come on this trip?' Linnéa was weakened by the words.

'The university was obliged to give him one last chance. There was no reason to stop him joining the group. We made it clear that this was his very last chance. Our best position is that he graduates with a pass degree and then we're done.' Erik shrugged. 'Do you want to know a secret? I have already marked his non-existent, non-submitted project dissertation. He attained a pass mark based on attendance on this trip and some limited engagement with the intended learning outcomes.'

'You mean he walked up Trollveggen with some survey flags?' queried Linnéa.

Erik said nothing more.

'Have you already marked our work, Professor?' asked Jonas.

Erik got up and placed his cup of spiced honey on the table very slowly and deliberately. 'Jonas Bjornskrom. You will trust that this old man in front of you, in all his years, has gathered enough wisdom about him to serve as your protector and defender against all those sent to try us.'

The students were as silent as they had been at their very first lecture at university. Then Linnéa dared to make a suggestion.

'Professor. We can use the radio in the boat.'

'Of course!' The others said. 'Yes, there is a radio in the boat.'

'All this talk of appeasing Magnus has stopped us from thinking clearly. We don't want to leave or end this trip, but now we must think of doing so.' Linnéa was bright-eyed and hopeful.

Erik went to the kitchen and returned with a bottle of champagne that he had hidden from all eyes by stowing it at the back of a cupboard, in a box of cleaning supplies.

'I proposed to my wife, Marta, twenty-five years ago, on Midsummer's Eve. In three days, at the height of our party, I will open this bottle of champagne. Upon the cork leaving the bottle, I will remember the combination to the locker, which I am afraid I have forgotten. After this has happened, I will activate the SatPhone and call the police for assistance.' He put down the bottle. 'That is a promise. I cannot remember the ridiculous four-digit combination in any other way. As we speak, my unconscious mind, whatever and wherever it is, has received my request, and will deliver me the answer as planned.'

'That's very nice, Professor,' said Linnéa. 'But what about the radio in the boat?'

'Magnus has disabled the boat. He must have done it during the last few days.'

'What!' Linnéa screamed.

'He took out the fuses and the starter motors and dumped the battery. The boat is dead in the water.'

Linnéa burst into tears. 'We're dead in the water, you mean.'

'Calm down,' said Jonas, but he looked uncertain.

Per was thoughtful. 'The starter motor is a specialist part. There's nothing else we can use to replace it.'

'Magnus took a lot of interest in the boat when it was lying at harbour,' said Erik. 'Do you remember? I was pleased. I thought it might be showing that he was taking an interest in the whole trip.'

'You could float the boat out on the tide, but that's risky,' said Per. 'You took us in against a great current from the east when we arrived. Without power, the boat would likely end up west inside the whirlpool.'

Erik nodded. 'The whirlpool claimed more lives of enemy soldiers than Grandpa Bø ever did, not that he let that spoil his stories.'

Linnéa looked out to sea towards the mainland. 'So the reality is that we can't leave?'

Erik nodded. 'Not easily.'

'Anyway Professor,' said Per. 'There is a simple solution if you are very concerned. Smash open the locker. Retrieve the SatPhone. Call the police. Let them deal with Magnus.'

'I've tried everything. I really have,' said Erik.

'So we have to wait for rescue on Monday?' said Mette.

'While Magnus prepares his next move, perched at the eagle's nest on top of Trollveggen.' Per saluted the sky. 'He really is the king of the mountain.'

'He is no such thing. Trollveggen is only a hill. Magnus is a piss-ant upstart' said Erik, surprised at the anger rising in him. 'He is a disgrace to the university and to his family.'

The students said nothing. All that could be heard was Linnéa's sobbing.

Erik spoke softly. 'You have your project work to do. Magnus wants to be alone. He will not disrupt your work.

I acted in his best interests when I allowed him on this trip, and that has not changed. I am in charge of this research island and we will complete the annual survey, as we have done every year.'

Erik left the table and picked up his coat from the pegs near the doorway. He put on his old brown shoes and un-locked the door. With a sudden movement he opened the door wide and stood ready to confront Magnus. The coast was clear. He stepped out on to the deck.

Immediately he smelt something unusual and looked down to see the bottom of the door stained dark brown. The smell reminded him of the foxes that visited his Tromsø garden.

Erik was unflappable. 'Magnus, you were sent to test me, and I will pass this test.' He explained what had happened to the door to the students. Although they were still in the cabin, they had already noticed the smell. 'Keep the door locked. I will fetch a bucket of water from the sea and wash it clean.'

CHAPTER 16

THE YOUNG MEN on the boat who had lost the turtle looked at me hard. 'What did you see here?'

I scratched the stubble on my chin and throat, getting lost in the fantasy of maintaining a proper beard.

'See? Here?' I dissembled and dallied with my reply. I knew little about smuggling, but there was a market in everything, including turtles and no doubt other exotic creatures. I could see the turtle just to one side of the boat, sitting on a rock underwater. Eventually, I mimed a turtle swimming. The men glowered at me. There was a net in the boat, a wide collapsible net hanging off a wide hoop. There was nothing else for it: I had just got warm, but it was time to go in again.

I stripped off for the second time that day and hung my clothes over the yardarm or whatever you call it. I took the net and dived overboard. I kicked away from the boat to where the water had not been stirred up and opened my eyes. It took a few moments to look around me before I saw the turtle on its rock. I had the net around it in a flash and pulled the poor animal in. The turtle was so heavy I couldn't lift it, so I surfaced and told the men to throw me a rope. Down I went again, having taken a deep breath, lungs on fire, burning against the cold, knowing this would have to be my last dive. I tied the rope around the net handle and surfaced. They had to drag me into the boat because I was so cold. One of them threw a blanket over me and through its thickness rubbed me all over to warm me up.

The other man threw the rope over the yardarm and started to pull. I hoped my knot would stay tight and the net would not break. Slowly the rope lifted the dead weight and eventually the turtle surfaced and was pulled on board. By then I had stopped shivering. Some people swim in a freezing sea for fun, I reminded myself.

The wet blanket was swapped for a dry one and eventually I grew warm again. I dressed in my blue tunic and beige trousers and thought of earlier times. But I would never forget today. The deep blue sea, the gunmetal grey rocks, the purple sky full of circling birds; this watercolour cried out to be painted in any one of several realist styles. Past the jetty were fisherman's cabins on stilts, their walls painted mustard, with white windows and grey roofs. Two kayakers in matching blue and red jackets watched from their slender yellow boats, the young man holding the young woman's boat next to his own, paddle ready in one hand.

The turtle was rehoused in a plastic box. This made the men very happy with me. One of them put two fingers in his mouth and whistled. The old chef cooking the fish looked up. I was to have chargrilled herring in a hunk of rye bread.

I approached the old man, who handed me a thick wedge of bread and two sides of filleted fish. I squeezed half a lemon over the food, the acid stinging the cracks in my fingers. Lemons for scurvy I remembered, and I pocketed the fruit. The old man raised an eyebrow.

I joined the other diners on the rocks. Nothing I've eaten since has tasted as good as that simple meal; the crispy fish skin tangy with lemon juice.

We all watched the men working on the boat, seemingly quite incompetently. A red and black animal of some description was the next to get away from them. It wove across the deck, evading both inept smugglers before diving into the water.

There was tut-tutting next to me. Someone said "salamander". Someone else said "idiot." There was no way I was going into the sea again to chase a salamander.

And then the woman sitting nearest to me said Sigrid, and her companion made a face that showed sympathy. I listened for a while, noting their body language. It became clear that the two women were talking about a mother's grief for the loss of a son.

All the portents pointed to Sigrid: she would be my next stop. I finished every morsel of my meal and leant back on the sunny rocks. It had been good to get away. My mind was freeing itself from the past, letting all the knots and tangles fall to the ground, where they might be teased out and the yarn regathered for fresh use.

The sky brightened and the temperature grew milder. I asked the woman next to me what time it was. Seven o'clock: I had missed the bus to Harstad. Fate had decided I was going to meet Sigrid, whoever she was.

I curled up in a ball behind a rock and napped a while. When I woke up my lunch companions had moved on. The black grill stood by the rocks, open to the elements and the birds picking it clean.

The two hapless smugglers of exotic animals had departed. The chef was now on another boat that had come in; the wind was getting up.

'I go to Sigrid?' I told the man who cooked fish for all comers and gave away some free to those who needed it.

He indicated that I should get in. No money was requested:

all he wanted me to do was wear a red life jacket and sit down behind him.

I inspected my inventory. I was wearing fresh clothes: slightly baggy beige trousers and a light blue tunic or shirt, unfortunately spotted in places with fish oil. The shoes from Bjarne were old, probably used by him for gardening, and the uppers were coming away from the soles, leaving my toes cold and unprotected. I still had the stiletto - I think that's the right description for the automatic flick knife. I felt that accompanied by the wolf skin on my back it made me seem a potentially dangerous person. I had no money. I had been robbed twice now, once by Bernt in the shack, more recently by Ramona on the beach. I had been without my passport since day one, lucky no-one had asked to see it. While not technically an illegal immigrant, I was travelling through this country living off the grid, gambling on my luck.

The boat moved out to sea. The chef-captain took me to Harstad anyway, where large tourist boats docked to fill up at the wharf. Eventually they would move off ponderously, heading to the open sea, and then swing round to stick close to the coast. I understood from consulting the captain's map, with a lot of pointing from both of us, that Sigrid lived a long way north, well past Tromsø. I shook his hand and said goodbye.

I was wearing just enough clothes to keep warm: I would have been lost without the wolf skin. One of my shoes had sprung a leak in the sole and the water was seeping over my foot as I walked down the wharf. A leak in my soul, I laughed. There's a hole in my bucket, dear mummy, dear mummy. Mother would be standing naked in the conservatory as Father painted her again. Good for them. They enjoyed each other's company and had done so for thirty years. I must send them an anniversary card; I was sure the date was soon. Friends and lovers are lent to us, wealth is lent to us, and for a lucky few it is wealth that lasts a lifetime.

Somehow I figured out which was the boat to Tromsø, at least I thought that a couple of old gents standing on the side of the wharf had pointed it out to me. The boat in question was a double decker, festooned with bunting. It was not scheduled to leave for an hour, so I wandered around the streets of Harstad and straight into a freak snowstorm. I slipped on the slush that was collecting on the pavements from the wet snowflakes drifting down from the grey sky. Both my feet were freezing now. I needed some dry socks; I would give my kingdom for a pair. These I managed to "borrow" shortly afterwards from a store which I had entered looking as respectable as possible, the wolf skin stuffed into my satchel. I had my youth, my smile, and my wits; Bjarne had been right about the way I worked. When I left the store, I anticipated I would be followed by a detective, but no-one came after me. The wind picked up and chucked some sleet at me. I laughed. Come on, I said, you can do better than that. I was two hundred miles inside the Arctic Circle. Then the snow hardened into hail and I was forced to be impressed by the power of nature as the icy marbles found my face and searched for my eyes.

In the main square I saw a reindeer drinking from a puddle. People passed by without troubling it. I was very taken with the picture it presented and knew it was time to practise my craft. A bin yielded up a clean and dry newspaper. Ramona's pen came out of my trouser pocket. Ah, Ramona, it was too short an encounter to get too romantically attached; it had been more like a good meal remembered fondly.

Sheltering under the awning of a shop, I sketched the reindeer as the rain came down. I had a black body, white face and marvellous antlers, dark and tipped with light. A young girl of about twelve or thirteen who was wearing a blue dress with a red neckline approached me. She had an embroidered belt around her waist, from which hung tassels that nearly reached to her leather shoes. On her head was a black hat with a red band. I quickly understood that she was the keeper of the reindeer.

I handed over the pen drawing and her smile lit up my day. She pressed some coins into my hand and initially I refused but I really wanted to accept and soon gave way to the temptation. I took the money and waved goodbye.

From a nearby café I watched the sky darken further. I immediately spent the money on hot chocolate as thick as soup. I had been given a spoon to scoop through the marshmallows and the cream. Come perils of the north and try to deter me. I am young, foolish and willing to learn.

When I returned to the quay the rain had stopped. The boat I wanted to catch was filling up with young people out for a party. I retrieved the wolf skin from the satchel and became an instant hit. Gladly I stepped on the boat: there was no question of my having to pay for passage to Tromsø to find the mythic Sigrid. I had my health, for the moment, although I had already tested it quite severely. Becoming a street artist was all very well, but a better plan would be to find a sponsor, someone who recognised the skills I owned, someone who would feed and board me. In return I would pledge allegiance and keep them supplied with flattering portraits. I realised I was searching for a new home. I was no hermit, or outsider; I was no bum. I was destined to be the secret weapon at the court of a powerful gold-giver.

Out on deck, the sea was high enough to toss icy water across the boards. There was some trouble with the engines, so we were forced to idle in one spot, bouncing up and down in the swell, until a black cloud of noxious diesel heralded a successful conclusion to the problem. While one's soul might be one's pilot, on this occasion I put more trust in the physical capabilities of the crew and their vessel.

CHAPTER 17

E RIK TOOK A black plastic bucket from the deck outside.
He walked down to the jetty to fetch a pail of water to
wash away the stain that Magnus had left on the cabin door.
He reflected that he was now well justified in his decision to
keep Magnus outside the cabin.

The motor yacht was nine metres long with capacity for
ten passengers. The hull and wheelhouse shone white. During
the summer Erik sailed around the coast in it and sometimes
took students out for day trips. He looked forward to having
more time to sail when he retired. He, Marta and Eva would
head south, travelling against the tide of tourists coming
north. For now, however, the stricken boat served only as a
reminder of their predicament.

He slipped the bucket into the sea and lifted it out, filled
with water. It grew very heavy as he carried it back to the
cabin. Mette was waiting outside; she asked if he needed any
help, but he said he could manage. She closed the cabin door
so that he could throw the bucket of water over the door and
the frame. He walked back down to the jetty to fill up the
bucket again and came back again, determined to expunge
fully the stain. The students had rallied and had emerged
from the cabin to carry on with their project work. After three
trips to the jetty, and now the owner of an aching arm, the
Professor was satisfied with his work. The front of the cabin
was gleaming after the water had soaked the sign-less door.

Erik looked round. Jonas and Linnéa were busy on their line transect. Mette was engrossed in her drawings of mosses. Per was not far away, standing on the shore and looking across to the mainland. Erik saw him pick up a stone, crouch down low and skim it across the sea. The stone flicked up five times before sinking beneath the waves.

Erik scrubbed the cabin door and its frame clean until it shone golden once again. The students commended him on his good work. 'All back to normal,' he said. 'Silly Magnus got caught short.'

Adversity turned to jollity. The students called to one another across the carpet of green mosses as if they were members of a predated species, checking that each of their number was safe and well. Erik had done his best to protect them, but they were not his children. If Magnus was seen approaching the cabin, they would all get inside quickly and hide away. Per and Jonas might prefer to tackle such a situation with a more physical response, but Erik hoped it wouldn't come to that. The art of a great manager, he had read once, was to brainwash your team into thinking they could perform at twice their actual level. In difficult times it was imperative not to transmit any anxieties to them. You had to look like you knew best and you had it all under control.

At lunchtime they preferred to eat inside with the cabin door locked. They drank coffee together at the dining table. The discussion was about exactly how many moss samples were needed and how long it would take to collect them before they could declare their projects finished. Erik encouraged their work, moving the focus away from Magnus. They ate a light lunch, more of a second breakfast: rye bread, jam, bananas. Per promised to bring some fish later in the day.

Linnéa remarked that it was nice to take a shower without the risk of performing an inadvertent striptease for the local lurker.

When they were ready, dressed in their coats and boots, they opened the door and fanned out on to the deck. Erik went first, Per and Jonas following at his side, and Linnéa and Mette came last. Mette locked the door and kept the key.

At midday the island looked serene: the colours of the rocks, moss, sky and sea seemed more intense. Trollveggen loomed even larger in the clearer air. 'That really is just a steep wall coming out of the sea,' said Jonas.

The students went back to their survey areas. Linnéa and Jonas began moving the line transect up the slope towards Trollveggen. Jonas kept a look out and Linnéa did the sampling. Erik stood on a boulder and surveyed the area. Mette went to her carpet of mosses and Per to the copse of trees.

Erik congratulated himself on having given Magnus absolutely nothing that was important to the project to do. He could toss away any number of poles and red flags and it just would not matter. He could try his game of rolling boulders at the cabin if he wished. The boulder field actually defended the cabin from attack: if Magnus had looked at the distribution of the boulders on the island he would have seen that. So good luck to you Magnus: I will sit here on the deck of my well-supplied and well-heated cabin, drinking my royal honey, while you shiver in a sleeping bag several hundred metres up a hill in the middle of the biting Arctic wind, in a place where only the kindness of youth keeps you alive.

Something came rolling towards him along the ground. He picked up the object. It was a piece of silver plastic, shaped liked a cup, with a hole in its base. 'Plastic pollution, even here,' he thought, then he startled as he recognised what it was. He looked up to the weather tower. The anemometer had been stripped of its blossoms and was standing stationary, despite the strengthening wind.

CHAPTER 18

MAGNUS SLEPT IN the cave for most of the day. He found a hollow away from the cold walls where he could roll himself up in the sleeping bag. It provided enough shelter to keep out of the way of the driving wind and rain that was penetrating beyond the entrance. The calls of the sea birds were becoming annoying: they would land on the edge of the cliff then step inside his home, shattering the peace with their caws and shrieks. He watched them peck at the ground for food. They left slimy white and grey droppings all over the cave floor.

He made a new fire, using a new technique. From his magical sack he took out what he needed: a nine-volt battery he had lifted from one of the smoke detectors in the cabin; a short length of blue wire taken from the dashboard of the boat; and a ball of wire wool that had originally been employed in cleaning saucepans. He wired up the battery to the wire wool. The metal filaments caught and ignited the tinder he placed on top of it in the fire pit. There was smoke, then a crackling, then flames, and another fire was born.

There had been other potential sources of fire in the cabin. While the students were outside waiting for the Professor to drone on about their projects, Magnus had been in the basement checking out what they had. He had taken in the usefulness of the diesel-powered electrical generator, a large model he had seen before in camping stores. He couldn't remember if diesel ignited or not on an open flame, but it was a possibility worth considering if the need should arise. Per kept his cigarette lighter on him at all times, so there was no prospect of getting hold of that, unless he killed the little squirt. Magnus had also found the propane canister that heated the rainwater that was pumped up to the shower and the sinks in the bathroom and kitchen. Magnus pondered all these possibilities while he warmed his hands by the small fire. Already this second tent of twigs was half eaten by the flames; he would have to find other sources of kindling and fuel.

His first meal of the day was a large bread roll dunked in a can of oily tuna. He kept his food on a ledge, although he had seen no ground dwelling animals. Next to the food he placed a bottle of lemon and lime washing up liquid. He tipped a handful out now and rubbed it under his arms. Sexy, he thought; Mette would like that citrus scent.

Later in the day he finished all the tuna from the tins, and all the bread. Some of the banana he had stepped on was thrown into the sea, but he ate the rest.

Thoughts of Jeong appeared. She had worked in a hotel in Malaysia, where the most sought-after room had three walls and was open to the elements. Guests, usually couples on honeymoons, paid a small fortune to rent that room. He had such a place now, three walls, a high ceiling and a sea-view. All he needed was a woman with whom to share his life and home, and he could play the part of the self-sufficient mountain man. It was all coming together nicely. He had the mountain and the survival skills; and there was a fine young woman waiting for him down there in the cabin.

Magnus climbed up out of the chimney and surveyed the island from the summit of the mountain. The students were at their posts again, working away diligently. What pointless lives, he thought. At least he had chosen his way in life, rather than being handed it. Didn't they know that they were clones, no different from the many other students who had come before them?

He walked down the eastern side of Trollveggen and sneaked along the shoreline until he reached the copse of trees. It was the easiest way of coming down off the mountain while keeping out of sight of the cabin. His guts cried out. Magnus the Great was a big man and he desired food.

Erik was climbing up the weather tower. Professor, Magnus shouted silently: come down from there this instant! The wind got up, blew right through Magnus, and swayed Erik on the tower. Don't fall, Professor! Erik had now worked his way to the top of the tower and was inspecting the anemometer. Without its cups to capture the air, the instrument remained motionless despite the wind. Poor old Professor!

Magnus watched Erik take a key from his pocket. He used it to open the door to the environmental enclosure that housed the control box. Magnus remembered the feel of the wires and the many connections he had disrupted. The Professor worked on the tangled mess inside the box until he was satisfied with his repairs. Linnéa appeared with a towel and a bottle of water, and she took them to clean the soil off the solar radiation sensor.

Per was up ahead on the rocks, casting a big black rod and line out to sea. He was good at fishing. Magnus watched as the line dipped once and then bowed more deeply. Per reeled in the catch, taking his time, walking along the rocks, bringing the fish into the shore where one of the black buckets waited. It would be easy to dispense with Per, but no one else had his talent for catching fish.

Magnus suddenly thought of a joke. Teach a man to fish and you feed a thief for life!

Another lightbulb went off in his head. He had trouble integrating with polite company, so maybe jokes and humour were his way ahead. He could buy a book on jokes and memorise them. People liked jokes. Mette would certainly like a partner with a good sense of humour. People questioned the emotional intelligence of Magnus the Great, but, really, he was a genius.

How to separate Per from the bucket of fish was the immediate problem. Magnus waited behind one of the few trees on the island. He conjured up diversions in his mind. A stone thrown over on to the survey area, or at the cabin or near the tower would be a distraction. But any one of the students could immediately back-track along the stone's trajectory and spot Magnus near the copse of trees. And it would be an act of war, a deliberate missile attack, which he wasn't quite ready for. He should attack from a position of strength, from high ground, with overwhelming force. Or attack at night, using the element of surprise. The last seemed like a good plan and one that grew and bubbled in his brain as much as his stomach and guts rumbled.

In the end he didn't need to steal any fish. Per collected up his bucket and rod and went back to the cabin. He brought out a bag of charcoal and dumped it on the brick surround. Linnéa came out with a metal grill, wiped it clean, and placed it on the bricks. Per produced his lighter, which was what Magnus really wanted, and lit the charcoal bag. Grey smoke appeared as the bag flaked and disintegrated; soon orange flames emerged.

Patience was what Magnus learnt that evening. He was

hidden in the copse of trees wearing his grey rain jacket and leaning back against the yellow- and grey-streaked rocks. He was resting on a cushion of mosses, which kept him warm and dry. When the students came in or out of their cabin there was always someone on guard. At the moment the lookouts were Jonas and Mette. She was sitting on the deck in the Professor's chair. Her line of vision took in the whole of Trollveggen and the impossible western route around the low coastline to the jetty. Jonas stood next to her. He was covering the high ground and the central approach down through the boulder field.

The students ate well that evening. The smell of fried fish tormented Magnus. His mouth welled up and fell open. He drooled over his clapped-out boots as he leant against the rocks and his stomach ached with hunger. Per was the man, the bringer of fish; he sustained life. Magnus whimpered a little and then checked himself, concerned that Erik and the students would hear his guts crying out for food.

He distracted himself with practical thoughts of survival. He needed wood for a fire to cook any fish he might steal: a bird's nest wouldn't do at all. Magnus inspected the trees for a likely source. He saw where Per had been working. Great slabs of moss had been scalped off one particular tree. On another tree, perhaps where Per had stood to reach up higher, a branch was half broken and sagging to the ground. He produced his flick-knife and cut into the wood until the branch dropped silently into his hands.

Then he saw the apple tree. What a beauty! It was in blossom. Just for a moment, he felt quite strange. Prior to this, only looking at Jeong or Mette had produced any such feelings in him. Why was this tree beautiful? He couldn't figure it out.

When most of the world was dark and grey, why did a simple tree with white and yellow blossom affect him so much?

When he looked back at the cabin he saw Mette carrying out another white bag. She left it on the first boulder, as she had left the first one. His happy thoughts faded. Magnus the Great did not accept charity, not even from the beautiful Mette, and not even if he was starving. He trusted her, of course, but what if one of the others had poisoned the food before she left it out?

Mette went inside and closed the cabin door. Magnus waited for a few minutes, then he set down the tree branch and walked boldly towards the cabin and the smoking grill. He crept along silently, taking advantage of his large stride to cover the distance quickly, listening intently for the cabin door to open again. There was not even a twitching of the curtains. Out of sight was out of mind as far as the other students were concerned. They had written off Magnus.

There were scraps of fish left on the grill. He picked the pieces off with his fingers, ignoring the heat as he pulled at the white flesh seared and smoking on the metal bars. With his appetite inflamed, he picked up the grill and licked the burnt fish off the metal grid until his tongue was on fire. The hot metal bars burnt his fingers, but the taste was so good he didn't care.

When he had picked the grill clean he placed it carefully on the brick surround and returned to the copse of trees. He picked up the tree branch and balanced it on his shoulder. He was ready to take the long eastern coastal route home again. A cracking and smashing sound from the cabin made him stop and turn around. He stood still against the rocks patterned with yellow, green and black mosses and watched the fun.

The students had dragged out a long green rectangular container on to the deck outside the cabin. Per went first and hit it with a hammer. Magnus frowned. He was unaware that they had the hammer. He would very much like to have a hammer.

Magnus watched while the Professor and the students hit and smashed at the locker. He heard their shouting and Linnéa's crying when the locker refused to give up its contents. He saw their faces turn to look up, pleading, towards Trollveggen, but he knew he was invisible in the twilight. Turn your faces heavenwards, and worship the true king, Magnus the Great!

Linnéa walked away down to the jetty. She was crying like a bird. The strikes of the hammer rang out again as Per gave it everything he had. Jonas, tall in his orange coat, followed Linnéa to the boat. The Professor, distinctive in his green jacket and blue trousers, also pointed at the boat and then along the coast to something in the sea.

She walked back to the cabin with Jonas' arm around her shoulder. There was no escape that way. You, who have everything, thought Magnus, do not deserve one thing more.

Linnéa started shouting at Erik. The Professor could not remember the combination to the padlock! He was endangering all of them! How could he do that? How could the university put her in such a position? She went into the cabin sobbing.

Per and Jonas, and then Erik, tried again with the locker, but the hammer made no impression. The locker was impregnable. In the end they gave up and dragged it back inside.

Magnus was up on his feet, delighted, a broad smile across his face. They fear me! They really do! He was ecstatic.

When he got to the cave he shimmied down the chimney in record time. He told his mother all about the satellite phone that could summon the police, the army, the navy, the United Nations, anyone and everyone to this island. The authorities would storm their cosy cave on Trollveggen, and then the evil Magnus would be captured and locked away by his persecutors. Except there was only one problem: they couldn't open the locker to get to the SatPhone!

His mother was at first disbelieving; then, when she realised what had happened, she joined in his laughter. But they know a lot about mosses, he said, and she laughed even harder. He jumped with glee and danced with her. He put his arms around her bony frame and kissed her. They would celebrate their tormentors' agony tonight with a wonderful fire.

He made a pile of short thick sticks, and then another pile of longer wider sticks. He took the bark of a stick and scraped fine kindling into a pile. The battery short-circuited in the wire wool, the kindling took, and wisps of smoke appeared. He placed thin then thick sticks on the pile and grew the fire into a roaring orange ball. The rest of the tree branch was snapped into pieces ready for later. What a fire he made! He watched the thick dark smoke disappear out of the chimney.

With his chalk he crossed another day off the wall. His mother cheered him up even more when she said that the students were panicking. A summer storm rolled across the island. Her words and the thunder and lightning gave him strength.

CHAPTER 19

'WHAT WEATHER!' SAID Linnéa. She looked out of the windows, which were streaked with rain. 'Did you hear the storm last night?'

'It certainly cleared the air. I watched the lightning for a while. It lit up the dormitory. Threw some strange shapes on the wall.' Jonas was looking at the weather data on the computer.

'At least the dormitory smells better now.' Per sipped from his mug of coffee. 'No rotting Magnus. Instead there is the delightful fragrance of lavender and thyme.'

'Watch out,' said Linnéa. 'If you find petals under your pillow you will know what it means.'

'Oh, I'll watch out,' said Per.

Jonas was peering at the screen. 'There are some anomalies in the weather data. I presume Magnus is at the back of it?'

Erik came over to have a look. 'We have lost days of climate data. We cannot use any of it. The data is not to be trusted given that we know he interfered with the equipment.' Standing at the window, Erik looked up at Trollveggen.

'Magnus must have had a terrible time in the storm.' Mette had dressed and was heading outside.

'I don't think so,' said Jonas. 'There was no break in that column of smoke for hours.'

'I'm surprised, Jonas, that you can be so cruel.' Mette unlocked the cabin door.

'Wait. I'll go with you,' said Per. 'He might be outside.'

'Magnus brought it on himself,' said Linnéa. 'He chose to leave the group.'

'But he's not well, is he? He thinks he is strong, but he is vulnerable to making bad decisions,' said Mette.

'He's well enough to damage the tower, disable the boat, piss on the door, wreck the crest, and steal Per's boots,' said Jonas. 'He has skills. He knows what he's doing.' He pointed out of the window. 'Look!'

They crowded round the window to look at a new column of dark smoke emerge from the summit of Trollveggen. 'See,' said Jonas. 'He has made another fire. That is a difficult art; he hasn't done it by accident. Magnus knows how to survive. He's not a mental patient doomed to die in Bø's cave.'

'You make a good point,' said Erik. 'He seems to know what he's doing. We will have to make the best of our life here until Dr Jensson arrives on Monday.' He touched the frame of the photograph of his ancestors. 'Remember, compared to the past we have it very easy.'

'I don't know,' said Linnéa. 'I mean, there is something seriously wrong with this guy and nobody else seems bothered by it. Yes, he wants to live on his own, but is that all? What else does he want?'

'He has all he needs,' said Jonas. 'Food, shelter, fire, water.'

'Not that again,' said Linnéa. 'You say he has skills but then you are happy to treat him like an animal who is content to live in a cave for ever. His food, our food, will run out. Our bottled water will run out. The fuel for his fire will run out. Winter will arrive. What will he do then?'

'I agree with you, Linnéa,' said Erik. 'Magnus will face some difficult choices when the conditions change. But on

Monday, if not before, we will be back in Tromsø and this adventure will all be over. So far, Magnus has been antisocial, but he has not tried to harm any of us.'

Erik didn't tell them any more. He didn't mention how, when he had walked around the cabin, checking that the trapdoor to the basement was closed, and that the windows were secure from outside, he had found something pointing out of the wall by the dormitory window. It was a stick with a bird's feathers pushed into one end: a primitive arrow. There was no head, no metal point, just the blunt end of the stick, which had been wedged between the wooden boards of the wall. The feathers were grey and looked as if they were from a sea bird. Erik had pulled off the feathers and snapped the stick in two. Then he had scattered the components amongst the rocks behind the cabin.

Erik went into the kitchen and made himself another mug of spiced honey. When he came back Jonas and Linnéa were looking over the climate data again.

'Professor?' asked Linnéa, 'isn't all that honey bad for your teeth.'

Erik opened his mouth and showed off his white teeth. 'For some reason, my teeth are excellent.' He put on his coat and boots and went outside. A column of smoke hung over the summit of Trollveggen. There was no other obvious sign of Magnus. People are at liberty to live their lives as long as they don't harm others. So far, Magnus had harmed only things. Settling in his chair, Erik was soon engrossed in a review article and was a little peeved that none of his papers had been cited. The editor of the journal was well known to him; he would have to have a word.

Jonas and Linnéa emerged from the cabin as Erik was

getting up to prepare lunch. Midsummer's Eve, a day of celebration, was approaching, although no-one had mentioned it. If only he could remember that stupid combination it would lift everyone's mood, but he was tired from trying.

He threw items for lunch into the picnic basket Marta had bought in Amsterdam. He locked the cabin door, took a few steps forward, put down the basket, and returned to double check the door again. They had two days to go, and what a day today would be. Midsummer's Eve was one of his favourite times of year. They would build a bonfire and celebrate with good food and drink. On Monday the university boat with Dr Jensen at the helm would arrive with fresh supplies and a radio to tell the world what had happened on Svindel. Magnus would be found and taken away.

He realised with regret that this really would be his last field trip. To navigate himself and the students through this week had been very stressful and it wasn't over yet. He felt that he'd shown himself up: he was weak in body and in mind. The time had come to step down and let a younger person carry on.

He carried out the wicker basket and walked up to where Jonas and Linnéa were struggling to take samples from the furthest reaches of their line transect. Identification of mosses was always harder in the wet. He waved to them to stop. Now that it was time for lunch, they could break off their competition to be the best student; perhaps they might actually relax a little and enjoy each other's company. Erik reminded himself to tell them the story about the sleeping queen who lived on the mainland.

Erik and Jonas were approaching the fishing rocks and were surprised to see that the line attached to Per's fishing rod, which he had propped up between two rocks, was straining with a catch. Jonas picked up the rod and reeled in the silver fish.

'The man's a genius,' said Jonas. 'He doesn't even need to be present to catch a fish.' He unhooked the fish and put it in the bucket of sea water, covering it with the lid. It jumped and flapped once, but then lay still.

They waited a while. It was one o'clock by Erik's watch. He looked up Trollveggen. The smoke had disappeared. 'Has anyone seen any sign of Magnus?' he asked.

Jonas shook his head. 'He's probably asleep. If he comes out at all it will be at night, when we are safe in the cabin.'

'What if he attacks us right now?' asked Linnéa, who had just joined them.

'Then we defend ourselves,' said Erik. 'We are five, he is one, and he will have gone too far.'

'Saturday, Sunday, Monday,' said Linnéa, counting the days off on her fingers. 'Then the nightmare is over.'

'Has it really been that bad?' Erik was dismayed.

Linnéa laughed. 'I haven't slept properly since Magnus left. I keep thinking he will turn up again.'

'The cabin is our fortress,' Erik said. 'Please remember to keep the door locked when we are outside. There is nothing for Magnus to steal out here, apart from hot coals, and perhaps we are doing him a favour by allowing him the gift of heat.'

Mette emerged from behind a rock. She looked somewhat bashful. Per turned up a moment later, similarly embarrassed.

'Are we all here?' she asked.

'Apart from our troll,' said Jonas.

Mette walked away to stand on a rock, formed her hands into a funnel around her mouth, and called out to Magnus.

Her voice sounded like a bell ringing out across the rocks and foothills. The melody rolled up Trollveggen and vanished into the air.

'That's a very sweet thing to do,' said Linnéa, 'but maybe a little dangerous. Magnus is right above our heads.'

'How we treat those who need help says a lot about us,' said Mette.

'And I'm saying that wild animals are locked up nice and safe in a zoo,' returned Linnéa.

Erik spread out a couple of camping mats on the set of rocks that, over the years, he had found to offer the most comfort, with the added advantage of providing the best view of the queen of the islands. The sea was getting up and they all felt the spray reach them as it pounded the shoreline below.

Erik passed round the wicker basket. 'Please, have one of everything.' They all took an apple, a chocolate bar, a bottle of water. 'This will be our appetiser before Chef Per cooks the main course.'

The blue sea painted its way to the white tipped mountains on the mainland.

'There she lies,' Erik said, and he pointed as he spoke, 'asleep under the sky.'

'Who? Where?' asked the students.

'The Lady of the Mountain.'

The students stared in silence.

'A scientist needs to have well-developed skills of observation,' Erik said. 'In many ways, he or she is like a detective, observing what makes the world tick, be it plants, animals, or the planet as a whole.'

The students were looking beyond the rocks. Linnéa was concentrating more on the hills, worried that they might receive surprise arrival by Magnus, than listening to the Professor.

Then Jonas piped up. 'The Professor is looking over there.'

Erik smiled and pointed again in the direction of the mainland.

The students peered into the distance. Between the mountains, a valley widened out to hills on either side. 'I'm sure all the men here would like to hike into that valley and climb up over those hills to meet the sleeping maiden.'

Jonas was quickest off the mark. 'You're right, Professor, the Lady of the Mountain is asleep, or else she is waiting for someone. There is another valley to the left, beyond one set of hills and the next.'

'I can't see anything,' said Linnéa.

Jonas pointed to where she should look. 'Look to the right, and you will see her head; imagine the black scree is her hair.'

'Oh, I get it!' cried Mette, and she pointed to the figure she could now visualise in the distance. 'It looks as if there is a woman lying down there from left to right; her legs are raised, and I can make out her body and her head.'

'Good,' said Erik, 'once you see her, she never goes away.' He munched on an apple. 'What shall we call her?'

'The Ocean Queen,' said Mette. 'We should present her with flowers, and then we will all be safe.'

'She's no troll, that's for sure,' said Jonas. 'I'd say she is Frigg, the wife of Thor, and the mother of Baldur the summer sun god, who has been up all night.'

'You sound like Magnus, chanting the old mythology,' said Linnéa.

Jonas was dismissive. 'It's just a good story, that's all. None of the Greek Gods were real but, who mentions that fact?'

'Magnus is into the darker stuff,' said Per. 'He believes it's all true.'

They finished lunch. Per picked up his rod and the bucket of fish. 'I'll clean these for tonight.' They returned to the cabin. Linnéa carried the basket, now containing empty wrappers and discarded bottles. Jonas took it on himself to hurl each apple core out to sea as they left the rocks.

CHAPTER 20

S EA LEGS ARE a wonderful thing when you get them. You can ride up and down the waves and your stomach stays silent and your breakfast remains intact.

Whatever the craft I had boarded, it was not the timetabled service to Tromsø. This took a more leisurely route to its destination. We stopped at many of the islands along the way to satisfy the tourist passengers. I fitted in easily because the wolf skin attracted a lot of interest. I felt that it gave me notoriety, like Byron's bear when he was at Cambridge.

Disembarked on one particular island, I watched two old men levering clams or mussels off the rocks. They put them in black buckets and moved on. Another man followed them and stood in the shallow tide, peering down at the beach. When the tide had gone out, he poured a white powder from a bottle on to the sand. The third man looked, waited and then moved on, following the old men.

When all three men had gone, I walked down to the surf and looked at the small piles of white powder. The stuff looked like salt, and when I tasted it the tang on my tongue confirmed that it was indeed salt. Why had the man poured salt on to the beach? Was there not enough salt in the sea?

I unclasped my stiletto and tried my hand at foraging on the rocks. My first efforts aimed at dislodging some small clams, but they were tough, and clung on. I steadied myself in the shifting sand by balancing one hand grasping a rock while I tried to extract the clam by wielding the knife in the other hand. I managed to gouge beneath one specimen with the point of the blade, but I couldn't make it go in very far.

I tried to prise away another clam, and another, and then a mussel. It dawned on me that the men had left them for a reason. As I made more and more attempts, I realised they had known what they were doing. My knife was no match against the shellfish, which obstinately remained stuck in place. I tried to capture one last clam. With all my might, now using both hands, I attempted to remove it from its rock. The tip of the knife shattered, the piece of metal flying up to cut me under one eye. Shocked, I dropped the knife in the sea. I blinked, closed my eyes, and opened them again to check that I had not impaired my sight. I could detect no damage; I felt I had been very lucky. There was blood on my fingertips; the cut began to sting when the saltwater got into it.

There was a sudden eruption from the sand beside me: something was pushing up from a hole. A white shoot about the thickness of my little finger appeared, followed by the edge of a shell. I pulled at the shell with amazement and some horror at the quivering thing that emerged.

A young woman approached: another Ramona, I thought, but no. For a start she was a bottle blonde; but the bleaching process had gone wrong, leaving streaks of her hair the colour of green grass. She knelt down, placed her fingers around the quivering thing, and pulled the rest of it up out of the sand. She was holding a creature with a short foot, long cylindrical shell and long white body.

'Is this what you want?' she asked. Her English was good; another traveller.

'What is it?'

'A razor clam.'

'Does it taste good?'

She nodded. 'Some say like scallops.'

She dropped the creature into my hands.

The woman pointed down the beach to where smoke was rising from a barbecue. 'You can cook it over there if you want.' She peered at the sand and shook her head. 'There will be no more. The tide is over the holes now.'

The razor clam lay lifeless in my hands. I was fascinated by it, but also revolted. My question about its taste had only been to make polite conversation. Scallops have never appealed to me, and neither did this thing that looked as if it had escaped from an aquatic horror movie.

She noticed the cut on my face. 'You're bleeding.' She handed me a tissue from her pocket. 'Take care.' She walked on. Two young children, a boy and a girl, both with dark hair, ran after her.

There was a crowd surrounding the barbecue and its one cook, who was a stocky man with a fabulous sea-going beard. I approached wearing my wolf skin and the crowd looked at me warily. Was I a criminal or was I a good guy? If you turn up to a party with a wolf skin on your back it's tantamount to announcing yourself as the main man. Another young man, who was about my age, seemed to like my look and welcomed me. Now that I had his blessing others crowded round. I could feel their hands exploring the fur of the wolf skin on my back.

I presented my razor clam to the cook, who inspected it, and said it was edible. He worked away with a knife, cutting at both ends of the shell. The white creature was split free, like a butterfly emerging from a chrysalis, and a long dark tube was removed from its middle. The man placed it on the barbecue for a minute or so, giving it black stripes on both sides, and then handed it back to me on a plate.

I took the piece of lemon out of my trouser pocket and squeezed it over the flesh: another pleasing moment. Life is easy if you're in the right crowd. I remembered how I was fed all the time when I was carrying out surveillance from the garage. At the time I was trying to be in two places at once, which had been a lot of fun. This adventure was also turning into fun. Yes, I had to live on my wits, but why not? When life gives you lemons, make lemonade. The razor clam tasted just fine.

The young man who welcomed me handed me a cigarette, which I accepted. He spoke to me in Norwegian, and then in English, and we just about managed to communicate. I stage-smoked the cigarette without inhaling. It is an easy and worthwhile trick to learn, especially when you have no idea of what you are letting yourself in for or what the cigarette contains. I had to remain in control. If I lost control then I would never find the passage to Tromsø and to Sigrid, who seemed quite famous in these parts.

For the rest of the day I stayed with the tourist party. There was food and drink, produced as if from some magical place, and I talked with Europeans in English or French as appropriate. I thought of home and tried to figure out how long I had been away. High on the to-do list was a call home to Mother and Father to assure them that all was well. They knew their boy was an adventurer, so they would not be hanging about nervously looking at the telephone in the hallway. The last thing they ever wanted was a namby-pamby mother's boy. I would call them tomorrow and afterwards enjoy the Midsummer's Eve celebrations in Tromsø with my new acquaintances in front of a blazing bonfire.

The evening began to encroach, and the beach got colder. There were knowing looks and some offers, including one from another woman with grass green hair, and there was temptation. But I knew tomorrow would be much like today, with similar opportunities, so I hedged and parried until the crowd drifted away.

My feet were crunching through the pebbles on the beach while I was thinking about scoring some dinner, when I suddenly experienced a slide in time, a slip forward as if I were part of a video that had skipped a few frames. I had intended to put one foot on the ground in front of the other, the normal process of walking, but for one moment I missed my step. What happened then was a blank. I surmised that I had been walking on air, which didn't seem credible. The next footfall was much heavier. Then my left ear closed as if I was swimming underwater. A dull humming began. My vision started to grey out. I was falling into a dark tunnel, the pebbles on the beach coming up to meet me. I put out my hands in front of my face. I imagined I must look like someone playing blind man's buff. A voice said: "I'm sorry, I'm going to faint."

Then I knew that I was twitching like a dying fish on the beach, limbs contorted by cramped muscles. I descended into a thought-less peace that was quite pleasant. My brain dissociated itself from my body, creating a kind of bliss.

My ears picked up the wash of the surf on the pebbles again. The beach breathed in and out, just as I was coming to. Words and memories returned. I remembered that my name was Alexander Clearly, and that I was on a mission to nowhere.

There were boats further up the beach, moored by the harbour wall. The largest one was covered with a blue tarpaulin. I undid one edge of the heavy fabric and slipped inside. My knees banged on a wooden bench as I felt for the deepest place in the space below. I would spend the night here, protected from the wind and the cold. The toes of my left foot were still cramping; I pushed them against the hull of the boat to straighten them.

That night I didn't sleep at all, just catnapped. I was disturbed by one edge of the tarpaulin, which had lost its rope and flapped incessantly as if warning its owner someone was inside the boat.

In the morning I heard boots on the stones: maybe a fisherman was approaching. I heard someone striking a match. The boat moved slightly as whoever it was lit up and lent back against the hull to enjoy an early morning ciggy while admiring the view.

I scrambled out of the boat as silently and discreetly as I could, which is to say not at all. The man shouted at me as I ran away, wolf skin flying behind. A stone hit my back. I ran back to the tourist boat, which was getting ready to depart, and clambered on board.

CHAPTER 21

WHEN MAGNUS WOKE the next day, the sun was at its highest point in the sky. Thanks to his sleeping bag and the fire, he had been wonderfully warm in the cave.

He chalked another line on his tally on the wall; one day to go. Today was Friday; tomorrow was Midsummer's Eve. On Monday, Dr Jensson would arrive in a new boat with another group of students.

Magnus took off his jacket and shirt. He tipped some washing up liquid into his hand and rubbed it under his armpits. He knew this trick worked well; he liked the smell it gave him.

A screech from the top of the cliff in front of the cave made him turn round. A puffin came barrelling into the cave. Blown in on the wind, it landed and wandered about, bemused. Magnus regarded the bird with respect. It was a fine-looking creature but flew like a clown; he could see it would be incapable of leaving. He took out the sack from his back pocket. The dark grey leather unfolded into a wide sheet between his hands. With a gentle throw he tossed the sack over the puffin and pulled the bird towards him. The puffin struggled once before becoming quiet. Magnus closed the drawstring of the sack. The other birds on the cliff edge took off. Animals are not stupid, he thought, unlike plants. No one has ever been able to prove that plants can think.

He laid the sack across his knee, took hold of the puffin

through the material, pinned back its wings, stroked its head, and broke its neck. He waited for a minute, noticing that his knuckles were red, not from blood, but from exposure to the cold. The bird was dead when he opened the sack. He plucked it, gutted it and cooked it spatchcock-style on the wire wool, which he had teased apart to make into a thin makeshift grill over the fire. He needed another battery and some more wire wool. He believed he would be able to get them very soon.

The flames licked the carcass, burning the edges of the bird and his hands as he raised the bird higher. The smell of cooking made his knees go weak. This would be some feast! With food like this, who needed Per?

The middle of the day passed; the clouds dispersed, and the weather was set clear for tomorrow's celebrations. One consumed puffin later, Magnus was dozing in front of the fire. The smoke stung his eyes; he knew they would be tinged with yellow and bloodshot. Some fool had said that the eyes were a window into the soul; his eyes were a window into hell. It took a huge man such as Magnus to be a true giant or a troll. His mythological name would be Sack Stuffer or Maiden Snapper. He dozed off.

When he woke up the fire was out, and he was cold again. He looked up at the chimney and expected to be greeted by five policemen with pistols, but no-one was there. What a good start to the day it had been, eating a puffin for lunch. He kick-started the embers of the fire, using the smallest tinder he had. The students would see the smoke rise again, and know that Magnus had not only survived, but also prospered. They would marvel at this until their last, terrible moment. He slowly piled on thin and then thick twigs, until he was cheerfully burning his hands. He piled on the thick, dry sticks which he had stripped of their wet bark.

He impaled the head of the puffin on a flagpole at the entrance to the cave. He tapped it on the beak. It was a beautiful animal and had tasted very good.

Water was now his next concern. He did not have any left and he needed plenty. How had Bø done it? He must have had a network of suppliers traipsing up Trollveggen under cover of dark. Magnus climbed up the chimney and stood on the summit, the true king of the mountain. He looked down at the golden cabin.

He could see only Per and Mette out in the survey area. The Professor was sitting in his deckchair, thinking he was safe. There was no sign of Jonas or Linnéa. Were they approaching now, sneaking up on Magnus the Great? Had they taken the eastern route which led from the fishing rocks to the copse of trees up the high cliffs? Or had they attempted the lower, and to his mind, impossible, route along the west coast? No, here they were now, emerging from the cabin.

There was a burst of activity, then Magnus saw Erik and the students walking away from the cabin towards the fishing rocks. Erik was carrying something heavy that he passed from hand to hand. Magnus' stomach rumbled; of course, it was lunchtime for the mortals. They would have to make do with cheese sandwiches whereas he had feasted on puffin; but they also had water and many other luxuries.

He had planned to leave the students alone today, he really had, but he felt a pang of jealousy when he heard their laughter rising from the fishing rocks. It was the day before Midsummer's Eve. He liked this tradition, because it celebrated ancient times and the Gods and the Giants coming alive again, even if only briefly. He had taken Jeong to her first Midsummer's Eve party three years ago. She had been fascinated by it, lacking any similar celebration in her own culture; he also thought that she liked him. He had imagined that there was a future for Magnus and Jeong, including sex for the first time. He was ready for it, but she had not been. She had misunderstood his intentions. And then her brother got involved!

Magnus snoozed a while on the summit. Who cared about a picnic when he had had a feast? When at last he had again propped up his immense head, it was to watch the cabin dwellers drag the few chopped branches from the trees near the fishing rocks to a spot outside the cabin. They scavenged every fallen branch. What would he be left for firewood – had they bothered to think about that? Together the branches were stacked into a large pyramid in quite a good stab at recreating a Viking bonfire.

Now the strains of pop music could be heard: someone had brought the portable radio from the kitchen outside. The king of the mountain scowled: how dare the little people sing and play? The Professor was relaxing his standards by getting into the party mood, and a day early as well. Tomorrow there would be dancing as well as music, the bonfire would be lit, and Per would catch more fish. Whatever they said, if he, Magnus the Great, turned up, maybe even managing to apologise, they would surely try to poison him again, or burn him.

He stood up and stretched his legs. Didn't they realise that they had just made things worse for themselves? They were clearly celebrating the fact that he wasn't there. He had joined this trip to fit in and look what had happened. He had been exiled. Reprisals were called for.

It was two o'clock. Magnus looked at his watch once more

and threw it down the hillside. What mountain man needed a watch? It was obvious from the position of the sun that midday had passed. He was warm, well-fed - thirsty it was true - but on the whole he was doing all right. Best of all, he was being true to himself, while the students, just look at them all, were standing in a sycophantic group around the Professor, listening to him pontificating.

Magnus laid another toxic egg and let it roll down the mountain. The fuming green ovoid rolled straight into the survey area and gassed everyone standing.

He picked up some boulders and used them as weights to test and maintain his strength. Then he dozed again under the sun. He called up a vision of a large man in the shadows standing over him. The man looked sad. In fact, he didn't look like a man, he looked like a woman in a headscarf who had been upset at a funeral. He or she carried the bells that rung the funeral chimes in his or her hands. He or she wore an immense coat that interested Magnus greatly.

The entire afternoon was one of the most enjoyable he had ever spent. He took off his clothes as Linnéa and Mette had done, but unlike them he stripped naked and sunbathed on the summit rock. He exposed his painful abdomen to the sky and asked the birds to eat his liver and stop the pain, but they were too scared of him to be beguiled.

The wind got up; the sun was still bright, but now it lacked warmth. He put on his clothes. He thought about the coat the apparition had worn: he wanted one just like it and knew where to get it.

The students had already been inside the cabin for an hour. They would be tucked up nice and safe. They didn't come out in the evening, for good reason. The evenings belonged to

Magnus, while he ceded to them the mornings and afternoons. Life on the island could prosper with such arrangements. It took him an hour to reach the high rocks above the swamp; then, carefully wending through the copse of trees, he crossed an area of ground that had been cleared of leaf and branch litter. The nearer he got to the cabin, the more frequently he stopped to check if anyone had been posted outside as a sentry or was keeping watch through the window.

He crossed over to the jetty, moving quickly and silently. There was a short ladder on the side of the boat which he removed and carried over to the cabin. Barefoot, he was able to tread quietly on the moss carpet; he avoided the gravel around the edge of the cabin. The curtains were drawn across the windows; perhaps those inside hoped that if they could not see the monster he might not actually exist. Carefully, he placed the ladder away from the window on the cabin wall and put one foot on the rung. The ladder remained where it was, nice and stable. He climbed up on to the roof.

Magnus lay flat on one side of the sloping roof and listened to the conversation he could hear through the open kitchen skylight. Jonas and Per were having a late beer; perhaps they had agreed to be sentries for the night.

'So we just need to wait for the Professor to remember the combination.' It was Per who was confirming something Jonas had said. 'He's trying to relax so he can remember, but he's so stressed out! You can tell.'

'Everyone's stressed out. Linnéa is cracking up. She won't even let me touch her.'

'Bad luck. You'll have to wait for the mainland. Or maybe tomorrow; it's Midsummer's Eve after all.'

'Let's see!'

Chairs scraped as the two young men got up.

Magnus lost track of the conversation when Jonas and Per moved out of the kitchen. It seemed that the Professor was in a spot of bother; his memory was failing him. If there was indeed a SatPhone, it was inaccessible behind some kind of force field that needed a special key to deactivate it. Professor Erik Nordveit was defenceless! He had no back up. He had no means of escape. There would be no cavalry charge against Magnus the Great, because the cavalry were on the mainland, unaware of the peril the Professor and his troops were in.

Magnus hadn't had this much fun in ages. He started picking at the golden yellow tiles on the roof. He needed to find a way to get underneath them, to steal the insulation materials. The knife his mother had given him was just the job to prise out and remove the tiles, as if they were the scales on a dragon. His hands slipped under the eaves and, sure enough, he could feel the thin curly fibres of the underlay. Slowly, he pulled out a piece, felt it in his hands and sniffed it. He thought it must be coir, made from the hairy covering of coconut shells. He lay flat on his belly and slowly and carefully pulled more and more of the underlay out of the roof.

As he worked, different voices drifted up through the kitchen skylight.

'Detain him for his own safety?' Linnéa queried.

'That's what the police would do. It would be nothing harsh. They'd probably send a psychiatrist to talk to him as well. He's not actually done anything wrong.' Mette was with Linnéa in the kitchen. Magnus stopped moving. If Mette had been able to look up and see through the roof, she would have caught sight of Magnus gazing fondly down on her.

'I wonder what he really wants?' asked Linnéa. 'Why is he here?'

'What do all men want?' replied Mette.

Magnus heard them laugh.

'Can you imagine?' Linnéa sounded horrified.

Mette's voice dwindled to a whisper as the noise of the sea lapping the shore became louder. 'Did he really kill his girlfriend?'

Magnus felt his cheeks go hot. He had wanted all those things, as everyone did, but they were all so difficult for him to achieve. And if they meant Jeong, they were guessing wrong; it had not been like that, not at first.

People should try a day in his shoes. The food he ate hurt his stomach and turned his guts into gas. He couldn't drink alcohol because the pain became ten times worse. He hated the way he looked: weird, waxy and yellow, even in his best clothes.

Shelter and protection he understood. He carried on pulling out the coir, which came out in flat hairy sections. He admired the strength and smell of the fibres. He saw how he could make a simple two-piece coat from the insulation material. With a hole cut in the top section for his head, he could make a sort of poncho to drape over his shoulders and chest. Then the second, larger, piece could be wrapped around his waist like a skirt, hanging down to his knees.

He understood instinctively what to do to survive, but about sex he had no clue. He had lain with Jeong but had ended up hurting her. And then her brother had arrived. He had fought him while naked. She had screamed all the while, and he had had to put her across his knee, and then her brother across the other knee, and then peace reigned.

Voices could now be heard coming from the deck outside the cabin. Erik was on the porch. If he stepped away and looked back he must surely see Magnus lying prone on the roof.

Jonas was out there, talking with Erik. 'I know you might think me cynical, but it's my guess Magnus enjoys being the outsider, maybe because it's familiar to him. I actually think he likes being the monster.'

'Well, I do not like this side to Magnus,' said Erik. 'We're living on a knife-edge here. It's lucky that he seems to enjoy the mountain so much that he hasn't actually bothered us too badly.' There was the snap of a lighter; a curl of smoke drifted on the air.

'I didn't know you smoked, Professor,' said Jonas.

'I don't usually. I borrowed this from Per. In fact, I kicked the habit five years ago. But this trip has changed that. I am responsible for you all, whatever any of you may think.'

The whiff of cigarette smoke reached Magnus. He loved that smell. He marvelled at the change in Erik's behaviour and was glad that he had caused it.

'We could go up there,' suggested Jonas, 'we could go up Trollveggen.'

'And do what? Talk to Magnus? Invite him back to the cabin? Tie him up in chains? No, I think Linnéa is right. It's best we wait it out. Dr Jensson will be here soon. She will bring supplies, survey equipment and another SatPhone. Then we can call the police.'

'No Professor,' said Jonas. 'You said that tomorrow, on Midsummer's Eve, you will remember the combination to the locker, and you will call the police. Remember your lecture on the Method of Loci?'

'Yes, of course.'

'Well, it worked. Every time I open the door of a fridge, I see a sunflower, just as you predicted.' Jonas laughed. 'The light goes on and there is a smiling sunflower. You reprogrammed a small part of my brain. I think you can do the same for yourself now.'

Erik was quiet for a while. 'I appreciate your support, Jonas. Yes, I will try. OK, then. I declare that when the cork comes out of the bottle, I will pour out the numbers to the locker padlock with the champagne. That is what will happen.'

'Thank you, sir. It is the best option we have to get this issue resolved quickly. The boat is disabled, we have no radio. Our cell phones do not work. No-one is scheduled to land here until Monday. We can listen to the radio on the mainland, but to them we are inaudible. In an emergency, we could take to the boat, but we would have to trust the currents and hope to get picked up if we hit difficulties. But Per says the current is away from the mainland, and it is dangerous water.'

'Where the Draugen lives?'

Jonas laughed. 'Where the Draugen lives; if you believe such things.'

'We need a hero,' said Erik, 'who's it going to be?'

'A hero who can fight a giant?' chuckled Jonas. 'I don't see any of those around here.'

Magnus listened to the Professor grinding out his cigarette on the deck before going inside with Jonas, who closed the cabin door. Magnus lay on the roof and looked up at the stars. He waited until there was no more talk coming up through the kitchen skylight. He silently rolled up the coir and put it in his sack. When he was done, and he hadn't heard a word or movement for some time, he silently replaced the ladder on its hooks on the boat and walked away across the boulder field.

Another white bag had been deposited on the boulder, lined up neatly next to the other three that had been left untouched. Mette did not give up. She was the only one worth a light. He picked up the bag and held it to his nose. He could smell a fish sandwich; it filled him with delight.

Mette! How could he refuse her gifts?!

It was time he told his mother about Mette. She was kind and was the only one whom he would allow to live. Or maybe Per could live, too, if he could be enslaved and put to work as a fisherman and a cook. The others would plot and fight against him and would have to go. Mother would be pleased by his thinking. She always said he was a smart boy, and now he was Magnus the Great.

He undid the white bag. There was a fish sandwich, a plastic bottle of water, an apple, and a bar of chocolate. All the bags contained the same things. He took all the items except the fish sandwiches, which might have easily been poisoned; a smear of faeces would have been the easiest trick to accomplish. He crunched through and swallowed an apple in one movement. The first bottle of water he chugged down in seconds. The first chocolate bar was delicious. He hadn't wanted to succumb to charity, but hunger is stronger than pride. What he didn't want to take or trust he strewed all over the rocks, as if the birds or other animals had spoiled Mette's act of charity, not he.

The sea that surrounded the island shone brightly in the dark as he walked up the central path to Trollveggen. The Professor, to give him his due, had done a good job navigating his way through the many islands to get here from Tromsø. Magnus had taken a romantic river cruise with Jeong on their last night; her brother had spoiled their fun. Magnus had carried the bodies in his sack under the moonlight.

He wished the students and their Professor a terrible night in the cabin. A night full of creaking timbers, strange noises from afar and glimpses of giants ringing bells.

CHAPTER 22

'HE STOLE PART of the roof!' Erik was incredulous. 'How did he do that? When? Why?'

They were all standing outside the cabin in the morning light. They had slept well. Thoughts of Magnus had disappeared during the easy evening of cards, beer, and stories.

Linnéa had wrapped her thin white hands around her face. 'He must have been trying to break in to kill us.'

Per laughed at her and pulled a stricken face. 'There's no way through the beams and rafters. He stole the coir underlay. He didn't take a single tile.'

'Why?' wailed Linnéa. 'Why would he do that?'

'It's simple,' said Jonas. 'He needs the underlay as insulation. The cave will be freezing cold and damp. Even Magnus would feel the pain of such seeping cold.'

'He was very quiet. No one heard anything.' Mette looked around the cabin. 'How did he get up on the roof?'

'I guess he came at night when we were safely locked inside. He's a survivor, he would have figured out these things.' Jonas shrugged. 'At least he wasn't looking for confrontation; he seems just to want to live his crazy mountain man life.'

'He's proud and stubborn,' said Erik, who had brought up a ladder from the basement and was inspecting the damaged roof. 'He needs food and water, just like the rest of us, but he will not accept them from us.'

'Have we still got enough water?' asked Jonas.

'More than enough. Remember the cabin is stocked to support more than ten adults for a week. And on Monday Dr Jensson will come and restock.'

In the distance they could hear the sound of chopping wood. They looked up at Trollveggen. Linnéa shuddered. 'God, please, no, he hasn't got an axe, has he?'

'Remember we heard that on the first day,' said Jonas, 'when Magnus was in the cabin with us.'

'Professor, what's on the boat that he could have taken with him?' Linnéa was wide-eyed.

'Spanners, wrenches, pliers, battery jumper cables. Nothing like an axe,' he lied. There was no need for Erik to mention the hatchet and the time he had cut the boat free in a storm because the alternative would have been to risk drowning.

Mette nodded. 'Imagine what it must be like up there for him. Magnus is living in a cave, in the twenty-first century. He's probably terrified and too proud to admit he made a mistake. So, yes, I will still leave Magnus something to eat in the evening.'

Once they had summoned the courage they set to work on their projects, planning to work only until lunchtime. From the survey area the view of the mountain was excellent. If he approached, Magnus could be seen coming towards them from a long way off. If anyone should spot him they had agreed that person should raise the alarm for everyone to run inside the cabin. It would only work if everyone kept within the survey area and did not fish from the rocks, but Per refused to accept this. 'I'm not afraid of the big idiot,' he said. 'He owes me a pair of boots, for a start.'

Linnéa and Jonas tried to get on with their work. Jonas acted as sentry most of the time, standing up tall like a meerkat looking out for a jackal. Linnéa extended the line transect up Trollveggen to where Erik had found the discarded survey poles and flag. 'I'm not going any further. This is his territory.' She counted the last sample. 'Hey, what's this?'

Erik heard Linnéa's question and he walked over to where she was standing with Jonas. They were in the foothills of Trollveggen, at the point where the terrain inclined towards the walls of rock ahead.

Linnéa pointed to a clump of moss-like plants with wide blue-green leaves that seemed to be covered in pustules. 'What is this?' she asked?

'This one?' asked Erik. He bent down, made a show of inspecting the plant, even though he knew immediately what it was, and why Linnéa had asked.

Linnéa nodded and looked at Erik expectantly.

'What do you think it is?' he asked Linnéa.

'A new species of moss?' she said, her eyes glazing over.

Erik asked Mette to come over. She took one look at the specimen, smiled at Jonas and Linnéa, and walked away, as if she had remembered something in the cabin.

'Unfortunately for your dreams of discovering a new species, it is simply a hornwort, or horned liverwort,' said Erik.

'Not a new moss?' asked Jonas.

Erik shook his head. 'No, just an old hornwort.'

Jonas was laughing hard. 'Professor! Professor! Look at me!' he mocked Linnéa.

Erik put up his hand. 'Making mistakes is part of learning. Mosses, hornworts and liverworts are the three types of bryophytes, so there is potential for confusion. Having said that, we did find a new moss here on Svindel once. The isolated location makes it an interesting spot for evolution to perform its experiments. Last year Professor Astrup submitted a specimen of the plant to the taxonomy committee to obtain formal ratification of a new species. It was confirmed by DNA analysis and now the plant bears his name.'

Erik offered to take a specimen of the hornwort and place it in a plastic sample bag, but Linnéa shook her head. She clearly felt deflated: in fact, she looked very tired. 'I got it wrong, Professor, OK?'

'It's not surprising to me that you got it wrong. How many mosses have you examined close up before this week?'

'None, probably.'

'Quite! But you've seen lecture slides and drawings of mosses in books. That's why we do field trips, so you can put all your book learning into practice.'

'I need to get a First for this project,' said Linnéa. 'Or my parents will be disappointed.'

'You are doing fine. Collect the samples in an orderly manner, as you have been doing. The most interesting results will come from measuring the levels of heavy metals in the plants when we get back to the lab, using AAS.'

'Silly mosses,' said Linnéa, 'I should have chosen another project.'

'Silly mosses!' exclaimed Erik. He waved his arm around, taking in the whole island. 'And yet we are visiting them here, in their habitat, and they are literally growing in importance. Have I told you that mosses are now being used to filter the pollutants out of city air? Yes, they are packed with other plants into huge wooden frames and placed in city centres to improve air quality. Silly mosses, indeed! How about the silly people messing up the environment?'

'Good point, Professor,' said Jonas.

'Cheer up, Linnéa. For a first-class mark, I and the other examiners expect to see you discuss your results intelligently, whether they seem to you to be either mundane or exciting. The results choose you; you do not choose the results.' Erik clapped his hands together. 'What are *Hylocomium* and *Pleurozisum* telling us about the air quality on Svindel?' He stopped. 'I could go on, but I will not. The theory can wait for next week, when we are back on campus.'

He went back to the cabin and disappeared inside. When he reappeared, he was carrying a plate of pancakes just freshly cooked in the kitchen, and a bowl of strawberries.

'Today is Midsummer's Eve,' he announced, 'and tomorrow is Sankt Hans, and so we must relax and enjoy life. Thank you all for coming on this field trip. I know it's had its problems.' He smiled at them. 'Project work is officially over!'

The students all cheered. Mette grabbed Per and kissed him. Linnéa and Jonas stood close together; they might have been holding hands. Erik handed round the pancakes on plates. Then he disappeared into the cabin again, to return with a crate of cold beer.

'Skål!'

They cheered and greeted one another. This is why I do it, thought Erik, to help the young along the road of life.

They ate the strawberries and pancakes. 'Professor, these are delicious.' Jonas was amazed at how good the food tasted.

'Remember, Jonas, the way to a woman's heart is through her stomach. With a strawberry on top.'

Mette ate half her pancake and then wrapped up the rest in a napkin. She looked over at the boulders.

Linnéa watched her. 'You're not going to leave that out for him, are you?'

'Yes, I am. We have plenty, he has nothing.' She placed the wrapped pancake in a plastic sample bag and walked over to the boulder field.

Linnéa followed. 'Not on our doorstep, Mette. That is just too kind!'

'There is no such thing as too kind. There certainly isn't enough kindness in Magnus's world.' She turned away, towards the cabin.

Linnéa called her back. 'Mette, wait. You should see what has happened to the rest of your gifts.'

The others joined her. They looked at the discarded food: wrappers and plastic bags had been rammed into the cleats and clefts of the rocks and scattered across the ground.

'Was this Magnus or wild animals?'

'What's the difference?' asked Linnéa.

'No, it was him. Look how he's stuffed some of the food into the rocks. He's like a big baby,' said Jonas. 'He bites the hand that feeds him.'

'He hates us, that's why,' said Per. 'He'd rather be hungry and thirsty than take our charity. Sorry, I meant your charity, Mette.'

Mette looked troubled. 'Why does he do this?' She called up the hillside. 'Magnus! Magnus!'

'If it needs to be repeated, then I will say it again. Magnus has a severe problem with people. He just doesn't understand the usual ways that people get on. He's a survivor, as he's shown, and he wants to do it all by himself,' said Linnéa. They all looked at her. She stood tall and brushed back her blonde hair into a ponytail with hands. Her slim figure was on show; no one could avoid taking it in. 'See,' she said. 'You all look at me, the party queen, but you know how to act. You know

174

there are rules, and ways to behave. Poor old Magnus doesn't understand.'

Mette nodded. 'Food, water, fire, shelter. But does that have to be his lot?'

They all stared at the hillside. 'He's found his natural habitat,' said Erik. 'If he wants to live as a wild man, we cannot stop him.'

'This island is not a paradise; it's not a place of bounty, offering two harvests a year,' said Per. 'Are there any freshwater springs, Professor, on the mountain summit?'

Erik shook his head. 'None at all. Dr Jensson surveyed the area before the latest version of the cabin was built: hence the stipulation for a supply of bottled water. She hates using plastic water containers, but there was no alternative.'

They made their way back to the cabin. Mette brought the half of pancake with her. Erik unlocked the cabin door and Linnéa retrieved the radio. Soon the mood improved as music reverberated round the island. Linnéa was the first to get up and start to dance, circling the bonfire Per was building as if it were a maypole.

Erik shook his head, smiling. 'Marta and Eva will be dancing, too. Shame I can't be with them. Like you, I am trapped here until Monday, when Dr Jensson arrives.'

'If she arrives,' said Jonas.

'Dr Jensson will be here, and she'll arrive early, at a guess.' Erik brightened. 'I will have to take my wife and daughter out to the best restaurant in Tromsø to make amends. Otherwise I'll be in a load of trouble.'

'So are we completely done with project work?' asked Mette.

'Given that it's a public holiday, yes. We will enjoy today.

You can think about how to analyse your data tomorrow.'

'You are the king,' said Mette and she kissed him on the cheek. Erik was so surprised that he blushed and Jonas and Per laughed. Mette disappeared into the cabin.

'Let's hope the monster doesn't spoil our party,' said Per. 'I have some respect for this guy. He's very sneaky. He stole the roof. He could do anything.'

'Some of the roof, Per, let's not exaggerate,' said Erik. 'A small part, really.'

'We could build a man-trap,' said Per, and the others realised he meant it.

'Yes!' agreed Jonas. 'We will leave a beautiful maiden tied to a stake as bait."

'Place her near the marsh,' continued Per. 'Lead Magnus to his doom.'

'Just keep watch,' said Erik. 'Enough of your nonsense!'

Linnéa turned up the music. Per started building the bonfire, with Linnéa's help.

'Professor, Skål!' Erik chinked beer bottles with Jonas.

'What does the future hold for you, Jonas?

'Maybe a year off. Lots of travel, see the world, check out the plants, and what can be done with them. Then a company job and make use of the knowledge. There's money in plant resources, and if I'm the guy in the room with the expertise, then even better.'

'The most exotic parts of the world, I hope.' Erik smiled at the thought of a bright student who wanted to carry on with the subject. 'I'm pleased at least one of you is interested in making this into a career!'

Jonas joined Per and together they placed a vertical tree branch in the middle of the bonfire and stabilised it by stacking other branches around the outside. Linnéa brought out a red ribbon she had packed for the occasion. She unfurled it and danced around the growing bonfire. Some things did not change; Erik and Marta had been just as playful in their youth.

Erik watched the soft waves approaching the shore. The sea was calm, the evening untroubled. The light was good and the temperature still warm. Soon the traditional bonfire would be lit; and best of all, he had to admit, was that Magnus had not been sighted or heard since the day he had left.

'Does Magnus drink?' Erik asked Per. 'We could leave him out a bottle of beer.'

'Not sure, I've never seen him in a bar. He creeps around campus at night, though.'

'I am concerned he is planning something.'

'Let him plan, there are five of us, and one of him. The cabin is impregnable, like that locker!'

Erik went inside the cabin in search of more beer. Hornworts, indeed, and a question about them, no less, from one of his best students! At least Mette had identified the plant correctly. He opened the cabin door and took off his shoes. He hoped Magnus was making good use of Per's bright yellow sea boots. Yellow boots to match his skin and eyes, Per had said when he noticed the loss. He was entitled to be angry.

He heard rustling in the dormitory and was about to call out when he encountered a strange sight. Mette was standing in the middle of the room holding a blue T-shirt, which wasn't hers, folded up and pressed to her face. It was Erik's own T-shirt, which he had worn every day until today, when he had put a fresh green shirt on. She breathed in deeply as she held the cloth to her face; then she dropped it in the laundry bin.

177

The next shirt she selected was black with a picture of a heavy metal band on it, the tour dates printed in white on the back. Erik remembered that Magnus had worn the shirt for a while before he'd switched to his more expensive branded shirts. He stood stock still and watched as Mette slowly inhaled the animal fumes from the T-shirt. She screwed up her face even more than she had when she'd sniffed his own shirt.

Then she chose a garment that belonged to Per. It was a sporty T-shirt with a silver dolphin logo over the right breast. Mette gently pressed the shirt to her nose and held it there. She inhaled once, and then twice, as if savouring a good wine. When she finally dropped the pile of shirts back into the laundry bin, she was wearing a satisfied smile on her face. She let out a purr of contentment.

Erik escaped to the kitchen where he made a large pot of coffee and brought it out on to the deck. He went back for biscuits. When Mette came out of the dormitory, he smiled at her, and she looked him steadily in the eye.

'I'm just going to try and text my secretary,' he said.

Now Mette looked at him in surprise, but she left the cabin without asking any questions.

Erik paced about the dormitory. He steadfastly refused to look at the green metal locker. The grand opening would take place at the climax of the party, before drink and sleep claimed the partygoers, after everyone had drunk an excellent glass of champagne to seal the celebrations.

He did not, however, want to look a fool. So he took down his mobile from the shelf and typed another text to Helga, his secretary. Helga worked on the campus in Tromsø, at the top of the administrative tower. He thought perhaps the height of the tower might help him to get a message though. Helga knew everything; she would text the combination and make him look good. He had sent two texts to her already, but both messages were greyed out on the screen. He had failed to send them. He pressed send on the third message. The spinning circle searching for a signal went round and round without stopping; he gave up looking at it.

The best thing he could do would be to keep the students happy, especially on this day of national celebration. He took out a non-vintage bottle of champagne, not as good as the one he had saved for later. The students crowded round him on the deck. The foil came off then the metal wire guard. With the base of the bottle resting on this thigh, and holding the neck with one hand, he released the cork with his other hand. It flew over the now roaring bonfire, to the cheers of the students. How had Per achieved such a magnificent bonfire? He really was a marvel. The orange and yellow flames licked skywards. Champagne gushed out from the bottle into the waiting glasses. Alas, no numbers arrived in his memory; he would have to wait until later.

They danced around the bonfire together, sang the old songs, and drank champagne and beer. Erik had a couple of modest glasses, but that was all he would allow himself. Linnéa's dancing turned to swaying as she quickly became drunk; Jonas kept her standing up. Mette and Per were firmly clasped together.

Erik rocked back and forth in his favourite deckchair and watched bonfires starting on the other islands. They sprang up as if in response to one another, a phenomenon he always enjoyed observing. Trollveggen loomed dark and fireless. There was no smoke above the mountain; he wasn't convinced that was a good sign. Erik felt a pang of compassion for Magnus, but then his heart hardened: he really had offered him every chance.

'Want to see something new?' Erik called over to Linnéa and Jonas. Per and Mette had disappeared off somewhere.

'Does it involve mosses?' answered Linnéa.

'Not at all; it involves a deciduous tree with attractive inflorescences of five petals, widely cultivated for its sweet fruit.'

'He means his apple tree,' said Jonas.

'I knew that,' said Linnéa. 'I'm not stupid.'

They followed Erik to the marsh. The line of two-metre-high poles had been reinstated. Erik went first and skirted around the perimeter, testing each footfall before placing the next. Some patches were soggy, and a few gave way, causing the brown water to rise over his shoes. He picked up a rock about the size of a man's head and tossed it on to a tussock of grass. The rock slowly rolled off the tussock and sank into the brown water.

So there was no Per and no Mette, Magnus was on the loose, and the swamp was still accepting visitors. Erik stood still and listened. There were still two days to go, and Midsummer's Eve might inspire a madman to do anything. Was Magnus to be the giant bluebird and Per the early morning swimmer? Erik shook his head. Was it that simple? A tussle between two hot-headed students? What was the prize? He stepped closer to the swamp and his shoe disappeared as the brown water surged up to his ankle. He fell back in alarm and pulled his foot free.

The ground around his beloved apple tree was firm. He had chosen the spot well. He was taking out a small paintbrush from a leather satchel when Jonas turned up by his side.

'Do you paint, Professor?'

Erik smiled. 'In a way, yes. I paint pollen. Come and have a look.'

Jonas watched as Erik dabbed the brush into the middle of the pink flowers. Linnéa had also joined them. A tiny dusting of yellow grains was transferred to the bristles of the brush and tapped off into a glass jar. 'I'll save these for my apple trees at home.'

Linnéa had now drifted away. Erik felt a little discouraged by the lack of interest shown by his star student. She stood gazing with a blank face at something inside the swamp.

Erik tried to attract Jonas' attention. 'Now, for the pollen from my own trees.' He took out another clean paintbrush and produced a brown paper envelope. In went the brush and the tip came away covered in yellow pollen. 'The trick is to find the first flowers to open.' He searched the tree until he came to a likely specimen. 'Then the pollen goes on to the stigma.' He gently brushed the centre of the flower. 'It needs to be repeated several times, until each flower is pollinated. After which, hopefully, the fruit will set.'

Jonas was grinning.

'Are you enjoying yourself, Jonas?'

'This is very interesting, Professor. Of course, I've read about pollination before, but I've never seen it in action, at least not quite in this way.' He kept on glancing over at Linnéa.

'I suppose that's another reason for coming on this trip.' Erik carried on, dabbing with the fine tip of his brush and carefully transferring the pollen on to the sticky stigmas of the flowers. 'This tree is something of an experiment, of course. I expect the apples will be rough and misshapen, but you never know, they might be perfectly round and juicy.'

Jonas laughed. 'Perfectly round and juicy is my bet, Professor!'

Linnéa edged past them and went back to the cabin without a word. Erik noticed the expression on her face was still blank.

Then Mette came by. Her face was flushed full pink, as if she had caught the sun, but the ultra-violet rays could not have been strong enough. She walked past them in her pretty floral-patterned dress. Erik, watching her go, tried to identify the blossoms. Another example of apple, he thought, maybe even a crab apple, with perfect flowers containing male and female reproductive organs. He noticed that the hem of her dress was wet at the back. She may have slipped near the swamp. No doubt Per had been there to save her.

'How are you doing, Per?' called Jonas.

Per was standing at the perimeter of the swamp.

He waved back. 'I'm fine, thanks.' He indicated the stretch of shoreline where he liked to fish. 'I'd better pack up my rod.'

'Yes, Per, you do that. Take good care of your rod. You don't want to scrape it on the rocks.'

Jonas followed Linnéa, who was following Mette, back to the cabin. Erik remained standing where he was, puzzled by the strange, silent procession. Per appeared and passed Erik with a cheery grin, carrying his fishing rod and a bucket of fish. Jonas had caught up with Linnéa, who was shaking her head; Jonas was laughing, indeed almost howling into his hand. Mette had to wait outside the locked cabin until Linnéa produced the key. Now Linnéa and Jonas were both doubled up with laughter. Mette was standing with her arms folded across her chest, waiting until she could run inside the cabin. Per motioned that Linnéa and Jonas should go in before him; he would stay outside to prepare the fish.

Erik walked further north, skirting the copse, then turned to the west and reached the swamp marker furthest from the cabin. It was a two-metre pole with a red-painted top. Here the ground was firm, and the grass had been flattened, perhaps by the stormy weather they'd had over the last few days. Mette's coat was lying, discarded, on the ground. Two sample bags full of moss from under the fir trees lay next to the coat. He picked up all three items and took them back to the cabin.

He did not notice Magnus watching a few metres away, hidden within the copse of trees.

CHAPTER 23

MAGNUS HAD SEEN the whole episode and in those moments he'd experienced the rise and fall of his ambitions. Mette and Per had found the driest patch of grass within the perimeter of the swamp. Mette had held on to one of the two-metre poles for support. Her pretty party dress had floated up in the wind and there they were; she was the fruit of his dreams, but she was nourishing another. He had imagined his hands on that soft brown body, his mouth on those luscious lips, but instead he had only been able to look on from afar. He had lost her to Per the fisherman - a skilled man of practical action, he had to admit. The man whom he had correctly identified as the biggest threat to his plan. The rock he held in his hands began to crumble from the force he was applying with his thumbs and fingers.

So, he would execute his original plan. They would all die. Even if that meant, though he was sad to think of it, his darling Mette. But a betrayal is a betrayal; it is an act that must be rewarded with death. Per and Mette, Jonas and Linnéa - they must all die. He didn't know their full names, only the Professor's: Erik Nordveit. Anyway, it was good to know their names, because it gave him power and would inspire him to do a good job.

He had known the name of his girlfriend of course, Jeong, but not the name of her brother. Jeong's death, while awful and genuinely an accident, had been clean. That of her unnamed brother had been messier.

Magnus had also seen Linnéa hidden behind a tree. She was being so nosy that he had squirmed with embarrassment. They had both been fixated on the scene in the swamp; Mette holding on to the pole, her body rising and falling; Per's underneath her. It was as if she were riding him to some longed-for destination that they had searched for together; and now they had found it she finally collapsed on top of him in relief. They had been very quiet. The rolling surf had made more noise.

What a lucky man Per was: Magnus could see Jonas' thoughts as plain as day on his face when Mette had reappeared. She had almost run away when she realised that she had had an audience. The Professor had been doing something to the flowers on the apple tree, Magnus didn't understand what: probably something to do with his stupid mosses. Linnéa had immediately walked back to the cabin, as if the end of the world had come.

Magnus was beside himself. Thwarted. Beaten. He was looking for a way out. He took the most impossible tracks home to his cave. He climbed up the sheer eastern side of the mountain, the one nearest the sea, the most dangerous and difficult route imaginable. His legs were hurting, his lungs burned; his sense of balance was tested with every step; he knew that failure would mean a lethal dive on to the rocks. He managed to reach the unknown side of the summit. Beside the great capstone of grey and white rock he then found something remarkable.

A woman was standing half-embedded in the rock. Her long body curved upwards; her arms were raised. Her hands were large, with pronounced knuckles and long nails. From her head and arms grew many tall thin branches bearing tiny leaves at their ends. The branches were twice the height of her body. She might have grown into a hedge if it wasn't evident that she was in so much pain. In the middle of her dark head was a perfectly circular mouth. She looked as if she was screaming.

This hidden treasure emboldened Magnus. By some feat of nature, a tree had attempted to grow on the very summit of Trollveggen. It was quite a short, stumpy tree, initially hidden from his view and invisible from the cabin. No doubt the Professor could bore him to death with botanical information about it. The birds must have dropped seeds into the cracks in the rock and by chance the tree had sprung up. Rainwater would have provided it with nourishment to grow. Little by little the tree would have pressed and squeezed its way out of its caged womb, until it managed to grow into a stunted reminder of the horror of life itself. It was his new totem, his new inspiration. Soon this screaming tree would be joined by more sounds of screaming.

Magnus returned to the cave, where he warmed himself up by wrapping some of the coir around him. He built and lit another fire. He ate a chocolate bar for energy and drained the last of his water. He would have plenty of water tomorrow, because tonight was the night. He crossed off the final mark on the wall with his chalk.

He hadn't been invited to the bonfire party, but even if he had, he would have had to decline. If a late invitation from Mette were to reach him, he would have to say he was indisposed.

He told his mother the swamp tale, and she listened

attentively, comprehending but silent. 'But, mother, never fear. I have a secret midnight rendezvous to keep tonight. No, I'm sorry, mother, I cannot tell you who I am meeting, although you may want to try to guess.'

He ate the whole of an apple, not wasting the core or the stalk. This was his life now, a life he knew had been awaiting him. He had enjoyed being a thief in the dark, stealing and wrecking stuff, but it had all just been for kicks. It had also been fun to spend the daytime outside his impregnable mountain home, watching the students and their master's silly ant-like struggles.

What was it all for, he asked?

'Mother, I need to dress for the event tonight. You were always able to make anyone look good with your tailoring, so now it's time to work some magic for your son.' He added another branch to the fire, which rose higher. The smoke thickened and flew out of the chimney, to announce to the world that the King of the Mountain was alive and well.

'The evening function will be a delight, but it's the finale we're all waiting for. I need to dress for impact. Something memorable. For however long those memories might last.'

From the entrance of the cave he watched the bonfires on the other islands. Brightly lit pleasure boats were passing between the islands. His time was coming. He had acquired the taste for cooked fish now. He needed more firewood, food of all types, gallons of water. He was the king and he needed generous gifts.

While his mother worked on his outfit, they discussed his plan. 'Yes, I've been thinking about how they might try to escape.'

Magnus told his mother about the basement underneath

the huge cabin. He had been there and seen all the supplies stored there. He had also noted the insulated line that ran from the weather tower underneath the cabin to the computer terminal near the dormitory. There was an internal trapdoor inside the cabin to the basement. There was also a trap door that opened on the outside of the cabin. He had marked the place with an arrow stuck into the side of the building, near the dormitory. He remembered seeing the trap door when they had arrived, and he had helped lower boxes of supplies in boxes into the basement.

How could he keep the outside trapdoor closed? They discussed padlocks and the metal pole with a hook the Professor had used to open the trap door, but they didn't have these items or know where he had put them. Finally, they chose an obvious solution. It had been his mother's idea: roll a boulder down to the cabin as if you are taking a pig to market, that's how she described it. Choose a boulder you can move, small enough for you to be able to control its descent; nothing too big, but not too small, either. Place the boulder on the trap door so that it cannot be moved by mere mortals.

He thanked his mother profusely. What a lady!

So he tried out the pig-to-market idea. He found several small boulders scattered around the summit that he could lift or roll for ten paces at a time. When he crept past the fishing rocks towards the swamp and reached the weather tower a little later, he already had a good idea of the size of boulder he needed to find and carry. The last leg of his trip was the most sensitive. He would be creeping about below the dormitory windows. He would need to place the rocks on the trapdoor in silence. The trapdoor was covered in small stones, which would need to be picked off before he replaced them with larger ones.

Erik and his students were partying outside when he arrived at the tower. He waited and watched. Per was stripped to the waist, dancing with Mette, who had his grey T-shirt gripped in her teeth. Per had an enviably ripped physique: a solid slab of muscle at his abdomen and egg-shaped biceps in his upper arms. Mette and he flirted and danced, and the T-shirt went around her neck, and then his arms, and then they were necking, then kissing. Magnus seethed as he boiled in the spray of the cold Norwegian Sea.

Jonas and Linnéa came out and played around on the wooden deck outside the cabin. Then they all danced around the weather tower, using it as another maypole. Someone had strewn flowers around its aluminium legs. Jonas, tall, handsome, strong, and a gentleman, was gently wooing Linnéa, who, like Mette, had changed into a dress for the occasion. The dress was white and soft, with gentle folds hanging from the arm; she looked quite wonderful.

Magnus flattered himself that he looked wonderful too. He hoped the others would like his outfit.

Jonas would be hoping to fool around with Linnéa, but it wasn't happening for him. She was nervous and rather drunk and distracted by visions of murderous shadows in the trees.

Magnus could hear her fluttering.

'My heart's going crazy. He could be watching us now, waiting to kill us all. Why did he have to come on this trip?'

Eventually the night air became so cold that even the bonfire was not enough to keep them outside. Someone suggested more beer and cards and they all moved into the cabin. The solid door was closed firmly shut.

Magnus made his move. He rolled, in stages, three small

boulders from around the trees so that they landed behind the cabin. The boulders rested on the trapdoor, glowing like trolls in the sunlight. He retreated to the copse of trees to wait for a while.

He was just in time, because the cabin door burst open again, causing Magnus to fear they had discovered him or tumbled to his plan. But it was only Per, who came out and headed to the bonfire, where he crouched down on his haunches. He had come to toast marshmallows on a stick. Mette followed him and passed to him several of the white fluffy sweets. Jonas and Linnéa came out again, too, and the music started up again and they began to dance once more. They were wearing their coats now, determined not to give up on the celebrations so early.

Erik ruled the deck from his chair and oversaw the choice of music. He just wanted them to listen to a few well-known traditional Midsummer's Eve songs, to remind them where they were. Jonas experimented with making his shadow into different shapes on the side of the cabin. His shadow was twice as tall as him when lit by the bonfire. The yellow and orange flames, tinged with red, curled away from the cabin and out to sea, shaking hands with other bonfires on other islands.

Like the perennially shy boy at the disco Magnus the outsider watched the dancing, keeping well away from it as if he disapproved of the fertility ritual it symbolised.

CHAPTER 24

I T WAS EASY to be a tourist on a tourist boat. I had the looks and the accent of a young man travelling the world. Today my part of the world was the Norwegian coast on Midsummer's Eve. We travelled in a curving channel that threaded between the islands. Our white motor boat had windows below deck that sheltered passengers from the wind-chill from the white-tipped waves. But I chose to stand on the upper deck, surrounded by young men and women in sunglasses worshipping the weak but ever-present sun. The upper deck plunged down to the sea, as did the small rowboat we pulled behind us attached to a rope, but we always bobbed back up again. I was proud to have sea legs, because if you dress up as a wolf man, you have to behave like one.

'Hei, hei!' yelled the tourists to the people on the islands we passed. Men and women looked up at us and waved; they were all dressed in the traditional red and white costume of the region and were piling sticks on an unlit beacon. We heard their voices and laughter as we came towards them, followed by the roar of the wind as we left them to their preparations. Soon we were heading away at break-neck speed.

Another craft approached from behind us, a blue and white vessel bearing the words POLITI. The police boat was coming in fast, its bow pointing up in the air, parting the waves into white spray.

Our boat slowed noticeably; the cold silence encouraged

some of the crowd to wrap up warmer. The police boat circled in front of us, waiting for us to halt. I could see one of its three crew members standing in its wheelhouse, using binoculars to get a close view of us. A policeman had been stationed on the deck. He had a dog.

The dog really brought it home to me. I'm not a big a fan of dogs, especially those trained to bite you into submission. What my wolf skin might have triggered in the police dog didn't bear thinking about. Behind me the rowboat danced around on the waves, towed on a long rope attached to the ship.

I wanted to continue my journey: I was having the time of my life. But Morten had probably reported me and if he had I would have questions to answer.

Reaching the trailing rowboat proved easy. I slipped down the internal stairway and smiled confidently at the caterers who were bringing out the hors d'oeuvres, making my way out on to the lower deck. The chugging noise the engine was making changed. I felt the vibrations slow as the captain turned into the wind, preparing to lay anchor. I stepped into the rowboat, swiftly untied the rope and let it drop into the sea. There was only one oar. I got going well enough, even though it was hard. I pulled away from the tourist boat as intended, tugging at the oar, pitting myself against the sea, as my shoulders seemed to catch fire. The sea was obliging; every swell pushed me on, until soon the tourist boat was some way away in the distance. The police boat behind it, so I was hidden from view, free to make my getaway to wherever I was going.

The sky remained light, in contrast to the sea, which grew darker. The surrounding islands lit up with the glow of bonfires; it was an amazing sight. I had no idea where I was going. It dawned on me I should be using a life jacket, just as I saw a red one poking out from under the seat. On the mainland, fireworks were arching up into the sky and exploding into stars. The coast was much too far away for me to be able to reach it, but I could see that I was close to some islands that had houses with lights shining.

I let the current take me on towards one particular island that had suddenly appeared out of the sea, as if I was watching the moment of its creation. At one end there was some shallow ground near a solitary gold-roofed cabin with a burning bonfire next to it. At the other end was an enormous wall of rock that eventually became a mountain. The mountain was shrouded in darkness.

On the mainland, more fireworks were arching into the sky. The sun, persisting on the horizon, gave everything an eerie glow. I was beginning to shiver, the cold damp wind cutting through my shirt and tugging at the wolf skin. The island in front of me was the only place I could land. Here there would be human company, food, fire and festive drinks. The golden cabin looked magnificent. I could easily play the part of a wandering tourist who had got lost after a heavy metal concert and had found himself adrift at sea.

As I approached the island I saw that there were others leaving it. Two young women were running towards the jetty from the cabin, one blonde, the other brunette. The blonde was naked to the waist. The brunette ran beside her. Perhaps they were playing some sort of traditional Midsummer's Eve game?

The sound of their voices travelled clearly over the water.

'I can't believe you spoke to the Professor like that!'

The blonde grabbed hold of the brunette's arm. 'We are going to be killed unless we escape. Don't you see that?'

The brunette pointed at the blonde's nakedness. 'Put on your coat, there is no need for this.'

'Then you can be Magnus' plaything. I hope he treats you very well.'

'It's freezing,' said the brunette, but she took off her rain jacket as she ran and wrapped it around her waist.

'All the way,' said the blonde. 'Mess with his mind.'

The brunette hesitated, then pulled off her top.

The blonde stared at her and then nodded. 'Come on, get into the boat.'

There was a long white motor yacht bobbing up and down at the jetty in the swell. I watched as the two young women undid the blue tarpaulin that covered it. The blonde undid the ropes fore and aft and together they dumped the tarpaulin into the sea.

'We have to be brave, Mette,' said the blonde. 'We are close enough to the mainland to be seen. There are plenty of ships and boats in the water. Look, there is one over there. We will get spotted.' She pointed to the tourist boat from which I had recently escaped.

'I wish Per was here. He would know what to do.'

The brunette sounded tearful, but she received little comfort from her friend.

'Men!' said the blonde. 'They chase like bees around a flower, and when the crunch comes they are useless.'

My boat landed on the rocks downstream, a long way to their left. I was concealed under the shadow of the mountain. I decided to wait to see if I would hear more of their story before I climbed out and made myself known. They were both holding a polearm and used it to shove at the wooden jetty until the boat eased away from the island and into waves. Then they were in the wheelhouse, pressing the controls and hitting them in frustration. Did they not know how to manage a boat?

The blonde went out on deck, pulling up her dress and putting on her jacket. The brunette, the one who was called Mette, joined her holding a mess of wires in her hands. 'Look at this,' she said. 'Magnus really is crazy.'

'He killed his girlfriend, and he will kill us,' said the blonde.

I was mesmerised. What hell hole had I landed in?

An enormous figure appeared and landed with a splash in the water by the boat. The young women screamed. I almost screamed. The figure was masked and wore some sort of shaggy coat. He grabbed at the side of the boat with his huge hands. The women kept him away with the polearm until he grabbed it, forcing them to let go. Something flew out of the hand of the blonde, turning and shining like a star in the air. It hit the masked man in the chest. He bellowed and staggered back. He found whatever it was that hit him and threw it back at the boat, breaking the windshield near the bow. He surged back into the water, but the tide was against him, already pulling the craft away from the jetty. The man hung on to the boat until he was waist deep in water; then he had to let go.

The boat drifted away from the island into the dark sea. The women were standing in the wheelhouse, hugging each other. I had never seen anything so terrifying. The boat left the island, trailing the blue tarpaulin behind it as if it were a flag symbolising the women in distress. The women began calling and waving at the tourist boat they had seen in the distance, but it was quite a long way away from them. I could not see the police boat; of course, I hadn't known the reason for its appearance in the first place. I was beginning to understand that the currents around the island operated in a strange way. The women in the boat were being dragged out to sea, while I had come sweeping in a current that would have dragged me even further from the jetty if I hadn't grounded on the rocks.

The shaggy figure turned to look at me. I froze. He was a very tall and powerfully built man. He reminded me of an old shepherd figure I'd read about, a man from southern Italy who scared children on one day each year, as a reminder to parents to keep care of them. The man splashed out of the sea, returning to the shore. I lost sight of him as he moved away. There was silence for a while.

When I had the strength, I climbed out of the boat and wrapped the rope around a large rock. The rowboat wanted to move down the coast, but the rope held it in place. I placed some rocks inside it to also weigh it down, and that seemed to do the trick. I peeked over the rocks and saw the giant moving about, his shaggy appearance back lit by the flames from the bonfire.

He reached into the soaring bonfire and pulled out a flaming tree branch with both hands, dragging it towards the cabin. My mouth fell open as I saw that the cabin was already on fire. He threw the flaming branch up on to the roof of the cabin. There was a hole in its splendid golden roof, near the front. That's why the young women had been running. They were escaping from being burnt alive!

The orange flames took hold of the roof as the new fire grew and eclipsed the old.

CHAPTER 25

E RIK WAS THE first to retire to the dormitory. He thought it proper that the youngsters should make their own fun on Midsummer's Eve. He could hear something moving outside and figured it was the bonfire shifting as it burnt down. He knew it was safely away from the cabin. He went into the main room, where the students were still dancing around with the radio on, and everything seemed fine. He drew back the curtains of one of the windows on the same wall as the kitchen and gave himself a fright.

Magnus was standing outside, dressed like a barbarian. He was wearing a headscarf and his face was covered with a mask. When he saw Erik at the window he moved towards it. Erik looked into his sick eyes and pulled the curtain closed. He went into the kitchen and retrieved the good bottle of champagne from the fridge.

'More drinks, Professor? I like your style!' said Per.

Erik smiled as he undid the foil and the muselet that covered the cork and he said: 'I don't want to worry you unduly, but Magnus is outside.'

The students leapt to their feet and threw back the curtains of all the windows. Linnéa screamed when she saw Magnus dancing around the bonfire waving a burning branch in both hands.

Jonas looked up at the ceiling. He climbed on a chair and pressed his hand flat against it. 'Professor, the roof is on fire.

I think the underlay is burning where Magnus made the hole.' He flicked at a white circular base fixed to the ceiling and checked inside it. 'Magnus has disabled the smoke detector. There is no battery in it.'

'Yes, he has been very painstaking and very clever.' Erik peeled the silver foil from the top of the bottle.

Linnéa glared at him. 'What the hell? This is no time for celebrations!'

Mette regarded Linnéa with wide eyes and open mouth.

Per put on Erik's boots and coat and turned the key to open the front door. Magnus immediately bounded over to the cabin and landed on the deck.

Per locked the door again.

'He wants that door open,' said Erik, 'don't do it.'

Jonas snapped his fingers. 'We can get out through the basement by using the trapdoor!'

'Try it,' said Erik.

The two young men rushed to the end of the cabin and down into the basement. They could be heard banging on the outer trapdoor. Minutes later they were back.

'He's put something on the trapdoor, it's too heavy to move.'

Erik stood there with one hand on the uncovered cork of the bottle. 'Over the past few days I have tried all the mental tricks I know to try to remember the combination to the padlock on the locker. I hope now, in the time of our need, my brain will answer the call.'

'What are you messing around for?' Linnéa exclaimed. 'The cabin is on fire! We are all going to die!' She pulled on her boots.

'Where are you going?' asked Mette. 'Magnus is outside.'

'Of course he is outside. He has always been outside, waiting for us.' She pulled on her boots and grabbed at her coat, before pausing. She turned to face the others. 'But even Magnus, who is a big, strong, scary monster, has weaknesses.' She slid her arms out of the upper half of her white dress and let the material fall to her waist. She reached around behind her back, undid her bra, and dropped it on the floor. 'He will never be able to handle this.'

'Go,' said Per. 'Run for the boat. Cast off into the channel.'

'Are you coming?' Linnéa asked Mette.

'Go, quickly,' Per told her. 'We will deal with Magnus.' He pulled open the cabin door. Flaming branches burnt on the deck but Magnus was back at the bonfire. Per put his arms over his face and kicked and carried the branches away, making a path for Mette and Linnéa so they could sprint to the jetty.

Per threw stones, boots, shoes, quadrats, and the Professor's deckchair at Magnus until he managed to engage his full attention.

Magnus roared and charged at him. Per closed the door, locked it and moved away from it. Magnus hit the door with a thump that rocked the cabin.

'They've reached the boat,' said Jonas, looking out of the window. 'Well done, Per.'

The banging on the cabin door continued. It sounded like rolls of thunder. 'I think Magnus could bring this whole place down on his own, fire or not.' Per wiped his smoke-stained face and touched his singed hands. A large piece of burning ceiling fell to the floor.

Erik carried in the metal locker and placed it in the middle of the room. 'One of the problems of being head of department is that part of your brain is taken over by so many meetings and responsibilities that there is little room for anything else.' He took the padlock in his hand. 'When I open the locker, we will find all the equipment we need in here to get through this predicament: satellite phone, GPS transponder, and a first aid kit.'

Another piece of flaming ceiling fell to the floor of the cabin.

'Professor,' said Jonas, 'you said that you proposed to your wife on Midsummer's Eve.'

Erik picked up the champagne bottle. 'We were in Sweden, in an ice-hotel, before they became fashionable.' He placed the base of the bottle on his thigh and held it tight. With the other hand, he began to loosen the cork. 'She was the most beautiful creature I had ever seen.'

Jonas watched as the cork slowly enlarged in the neck of the bottle. Smoke was now curling around the ceiling. It stung his eyes. He began to cough.

Per was looking out of the window. 'Magnus is at the jetty. He's in the water. Linnéa is fighting back. Yes! It's OK, they've cast off. The boat is moving! They're away. He can't get to them!'

More smoke entered the cabin.

'I remember the music playing,' continued Erik, 'the 1812 overture by Tchaikovsky. We play it on every anniversary.' Erik's face cleared. The cork escaped the bottle with a bang and some champagne fizzed on to the floor. He placed the bottle on the table and was about to dial the number into the padlock when he stopped. 'No, that's not it: it's something more practical.' He looked at Jonas. 'What's the module code for the field trip?'

'BO3312 Botany Research Skills.'

Erik dialled in the numbers. The padlock opened in his hands. Erik paused for a moment, then finally realised what he had done. Slowly he opened the lid of the locker. He began to speak, but his voice trailed off when he saw what was inside. Accompanied by the expected GPS transponder, satellite phone and green first aid box, there was a rifle. The weapon was about four feet long from the butt of the light wooden stock to the black metal tip of the barrel. It lay diagonally across the locker, almost wedged inside it.

Carefully, Erik lifted the rifle out of the locker and ran his hands over it. 'This changes everything.'

Per reached out for the gun. 'Professor, with your permission?'

Erik looked at the young student, his hands now blackened.

'Professor, the cabin is burning.' Per's arms twitched, but he didn't grab at the rifle. He waited patiently, breathing steadily, blue eyes clear.

Erik could feel Per's energy and frustration, recognising it for what it was: a controlled readiness to fight. He handed over the rifle. 'You know how to use this weapon?'

Per exhaled deeply as he received the gun and a smile spread across his face. 'This is a sports rifle, the type used in shooting competitions.' He tapped a black box on the rifle stock. 'Small-bore, point-two-two ammunition in a feed-box that takes five cartridges. The effective range is one hundred metres. Very nice.' Per patted the rifle. 'Very useful.'

He checked each component. 'I think we have Dr Jensson to thank for this. She is a sports shooter.'

Jonas's eyes were bloodshot and bulging. Smoke and debris were raining down on his head. 'The smoke will get us long before the fire does. We have to leave by the front door now and take our chances.'

Per slid the bolt in and out of the well-oiled mechanism and chambered a cartridge. 'If Magnus is waiting outside he will be sorry.'

Black smoke began to fill the cabin.

'We must go now,' said Erik.

Another large portion of the roof collapsed and fell on the cabin floor, lying there like a burning bird. The night sky intruded through the hole it had left in the roof; it was quite light outside. 'Magnus stole the underlay to weaken the roof to get to us, not so that he could keep warm,' said Per. 'I always said he knew what he was doing.'

'I'll go first,' said Jonas. 'I'll clear the way through to Magnus, give you a good shot at him.'

'Shoot to scare Magnus, to keep him away, not to kill him!' said Erik.

'Of course, Professor,' said Per. 'I wouldn't dream of harming a fake hair on his balding head.' He took off his T-shirt and wrapped it over his mouth and nose.

Jonas did the same. 'Professor, call the police now, before we all die.'

Erik took up the SatPhone and pressed the switch on the side. The display lit up.

'Red button,' said Per, 'emergency services.'

A voice appeared over the speaker. 'Politiet. Hva er din nødsituasjon?'

'This is Professor Erik Nordveit on the island of Svindel.' Erik checked the map on the wall. 'We are at seventy degrees north, twenty degrees east. I am here with four university students. We are under attack from a trespasser on the island.'

'No, Professor, it's not working,' said Jonas. 'The display came on for a moment, but then it went blank.' Jonas pressed the on-button again. The display flashed and then went dark. 'There's no power. It needs a battery or mains power.'

Per swore. 'There's no time.' He put his hand on the front door and pulled it back. 'The door handle is getting hot. Soon we will be suffocated. We need to move.'

Suddenly half the crackling roof caved in. Black smoke filled the room and nudged its way into every corridor of air, sucking the oxygen from the cabin. A dark shape was standing above them on the roof. Magnus looked down, his hellish eyes glowing in the flames. He was preparing to jump into the cabin.

'Magnus! Stop!' ordered Erik.

Per stepped out from behind Erik and raised the rifle to his shoulder, his eyes streaming. His finger squeezed the trigger. The rifle bucked up and the round cracked away. Magnus fell backwards and rolled off the roof on to the ground.

'Let's go, front door, NOW.' Jonas wrapped a towel around his hand, grasped the handle, and pulled open the door. He went out first, hands raised in front of his head to ward off any attack. The cold air stripped the smoke from his eyes, throat and lungs. Per stepped out on to the porch, ready to shoot. Magnus was fifty metres from them, standing on a boulder, his bulky frame silhouetted against the night sky.

Per called out to him. 'I will not miss you this time, monster.'

Erik held the satellite phone up in the air. He showed the bright green display to Magnus. Hanging from the back of the phone was the battery from the GPS transponder. 'The police are coming, Magnus. It's all over.' They could clearly hear the woman on the other end of the line identify herself as a police officer and ask for calm.

Erik walked slowly towards Magnus. At last his authority would be backed up by the equipment he had released from the locker. The rifle would stay Magnus and his steel-taloned claws and his stuffing sack. The phone had reminded him that they were no longer stranded on the island and that there were people to contact, who were now coming to help.

Magnus hefted a large rock and drew back his arm.

'Professor, come back,' yelled Jonas. 'He will catch you with that stone.'

The rock arched into the air. Erik froze. It dropped down out of the sky and bounced on the ground in front of him, catching him on the shin of his leg. He fell backwards, losing his balance through the pain.

Per fired. The round whined off the boulder where Magnus was standing. Magnus gave a leap into the air and ran off.

'No more, Per.' Jonas whispered. 'If he taunts you so that you waste all your ammunition, we are finished.'

Per lowered the rifle. 'OK, help the Prof, he's injured,' he said quietly. Then he shouted at the dark shape lumbering up Trollveggen. 'We will hunt you down, troll!' called Per. 'Hunt you down and put your head on a pole!'

CHAPTER 26

T HERE WAS THE unmistakable crack of a rifle shot. Hear it once on TV and you know forever afterwards that's what it is. The barbarian who had been standing on the roof of the cabin fell off it on to the ground. I stood straight for a better look, then crouched down again before he saw me. Was the barbarian hit, had he been killed? All was quiet and still for a few moments. Had I just witnessed someone's death?

The giant man got up again, rising to his full height as he bellowed at his attacker. He was weapon-proof! He ran away from the cabin, heading towards the massive boulders at the foothills of the mountain. He climbed one of the boulders and shouted and danced as he watched the cabin burn.

I found something resembling rope – it could have been the vine of a climbing plant – and used it to get a foothold to climb up on to the rocks, away from the water. The mountain man was laughing and singing as he stood on his boulder. I discovered a cleft in the rock where I could stand without difficulty and take time to figure out what to do next. My boat was tugging at the rock I had tied it to; it wanted to get away from the island and escape this madness. The midnight sun outlined a malevolent watery pull, an undertow, that was probably evidence of something huge and destructive lurking in the water to my left. I calculated my chances of survival would be better if I stayed on land.

I peered over the top of a flat rock and forgot how cold

I was. Three men emerged from the cabin. The first was tall and thin. He blundered his way out of the cabin, arms up as if surrendering. He was followed by a shorter man, shirt-less, and carrying a rifle. A third then appeared, older than the others. He was wearing a coat and carrying an object in his hand that glowed bright green. Was I witnessing a family feud or neighbours' dispute?

Some words were exchanged, but I was too far away to hear what the men were saying. A shooting star seemed to issue from the mountain man. It landed in a splash of flames in front of the first of the three men from the cabin.

There was another rifle crack, followed by the ricochet of a bullet. Something fell behind me on the rocks, possibly the deflected round; I didn't wait to look. The mountain man turned round and started to climb up the giant hill. I followed suit, having the same idea: to escape the danger. My face was smeared with a dark mess from the rocks on the cliff. I was a commando on a daring raid, starved and cold, my only thought to find some shelter. I heard the call of the voices of the men stationed near the cabin, and the yelling of the mountain man as he strode upwards. I recognised the need for extreme caution: I didn't understand the dynamics of what was happening, but I knew one shot from that rifle could be lethal.

The sky lit up again. I saw that the cabin was now convulsed by fire and impossible to save. The bonfire still smouldering next to it, which must have been built for traditional Midsummer's Eve celebrations, was dwarfed by the conflagration. The mountain man had clearly meant to burn down the cabin and whoever was in it, including the two young women who had already escaped.

What would I do if I met the mountain man? I stopped to

rest on a plateau and catch my breath. How I wished I'd never landed in this hell hole. My concerns about the police now seemed ridiculous. I was a young idiot, penniless, ID-less, but I was not a criminal.

Small rocks came skidding down the hillside, warning me that the barbarian was directly above me. I peered out from my resting place and saw a flash of movement as he headed upwards again. He must be aiming for some shelter, a tent or maybe even a cave where it would be warm. He would have supplies, food and water, all the things I needed.

Another noise intruded upon the night sky: the repetitive thump-thump of a helicopter's rotor blades.

The mountain man stopped and gazed upward before he carried on climbing up the longest of all the paths, the one that led to the summit. I was immediately below him with a vertical wall of rock above me. I had few choices. The safest place would be up on the cliffs, away from the rocks and sea, high on the mountain where there might be shelter. Fate had thrown me on to this island in the middle of a war. I reasoned that I was allowed to defend myself; I could take whatever steps might be required to survive.

I grasped at a handhold in the rock face. The climbers on the boat had already given me a tutorial in how to ascend a sheer slope. They had spoken about pressure and alternate pressure on the rock. The trick was to make a fluid movement between one moment of pressure and another, with no hanging around. Climbing was not about strength, but the flow of the climber's movements. I pressed down on a foothold with my right foot and transferred to my left hand, getting into a rhythm. I repeated the action, moved up, and put my left foot down where my knee had been.

I willed myself to climb this near-vertical wall. I was accomplishing it by moving like a four-legged spider. I repeated the action many times until I was standing on the top of the cliff. I didn't look down. The mountain man was standing on the summit of the mountain, silhouetted against the midnight sun. I could hear voices to my right, on the slopes below. The three men were attacking the monster; unbeknown to them, they were diverting his attention from me.

I walked to my left, towards the sea, where the wind was stronger and birds were flying up into the air. At the edge of the cliffs I saw the start of a depression in the rock and beyond it the ledge of a cave, where a fire was burning. I needed shelter, food, water, warmth. I recognised that this also meant that I had to turn round and fight.

I could see the mountain man, still standing on the summit, looking out over the island. Was he a native Norwegian, a throwback who had been disturbed by the men and women in the cabin? Was he fighting the others off? I could see that the mountain man was now protecting his home, while also trying to destroy his enemies. Maybe he had a rifle in his cave as well? That would be something I would like to take from him.

The cabin was now fully ablaze, the flames much taller than those of the bonfire next to it. There was a horrible screeching sound. I looked down and saw a tall tower which I had not noticed before collapse and fall across the ruins of the cabin.

The mountain man was throwing rocks down the hill side: I could hear the crack of rock on rock as he tried to hit the three men as they ascended. Tall flames were leaping up the sides of the cabin, illuminating the broken tower. It felt as if I had stumbled into a medieval battle. I half-expected to see a cloud of flaming arrows let loose from the hillside with the deadly aim of burning the enemy where they stood. Another rifle crack, much nearer than the last told me that the people who had inhabited the cabin now had the upper hand.

I was cold, I was shaking. There was a lull in hostilities which made me uneasy. I smelt the sea below and listened to the crashing waves. Their music might be the prelude to an attack of the falling sickness: off a cliff and into the sea. If I wanted to reach the cave, in which a very different kind of fire was burning with a low, welcoming flame, I would have to hang off the rocks in order to jump down to the entrance. It was a distance maybe of twenty feet, but it was my only chance.

I heard voices coming from above, from near the summit. People were shouting in Norwegian. This was followed by a rush of rocks rolling down the hillside. The mountain man was pushing boulders down on their heads! The rifle was fired again. The mountain man bellowed. Had he been hit? Some of the rocks from the summit glanced on me as the mountain man disappeared from view.

I swung my body down from my rock, aiming to land at the entrance of the cave. I let go with my hands, and for a moment I was falling, weightless, forced to rely on my own judgement. Then my shoes hit the rocky ground and my legs buckled and I fell face first. A little dazed, I picked myself up and found myself looking inside a huge cavern: it was much more than a cave. There was a fire burning towards the back of it. Suddenly I was slipping again, tumbling down the cliff away from the flames. I scrambled back as best I could, grabbing at the cliff for support. Soft plants came away in tufts in my hands. Small rocks were falling on my head. I was heading for the sea and if I couldn't claw my way back, I knew I would be dashed to pieces on the rocks below. This wasn't how it was meant to end!

Mother, Father, help me, I cried silently. I know it sounds silly, but I truly believe they did. I found the alternate pressure points and I stopped falling. I managed to move upwards again and climbed back on to the ledge. I rolled through some slippery mud and lay on my back, exhausted and panting. I could smell the fire burning in the cave. I could now ambush its owner aided by the element of surprise.

A young man's voice cried out into the darkness. He sounded hurt. Below, I could see two boats coming in from the mainland, moving fast. They sped over the waves; their decks laden with black-clothed men. There was a helicopter landing near the jetty, its white fuselage reflecting the great yellow and orange flames leaping against the burning cabin.

Every artist knows about moonlight on skin: you might as well walk about with a torch on your face. I picked up a handful of the mud on the ledge and smeared it over the mess on my face until I was sure I was caked in it.

The older man's voice floated down from the summit. He sounded as if he was out of breath. He spoke Norwegian at first, then switched to English: 'Magnus, the police are coming. Give yourself up.'

Was he talking to me?

'Magnus, stop this madness. The police are here!' He sounded desperate.

It was the thought of the arrival of the authorities that spurred me on. Up above me was a madman who had decided to terrorise an innocent group of campers in a cabin on a lonely island. Everyone at some point in their life makes a bad decision or does something they subsequently acknowledge was wrong; but a man who tries to burn people alive has surely given up any right to own property. The mountain man probably had a supply of food and water; if so, I would make them mine.

I heard the click of the action as the bolt slammed into place before the next rifle shot. This time I couldn't gauge where the bullet struck home. When I looked up, I half-expected to see the mountain man falling off the cliff into the sea; but I could discern no movement. Had he grabbed the gun? Had one of the cabin dwellers been injured or killed?

Then he appeared above me, at the roof of the cave. He was much more agile than I could have believed possible. He descended a gulley leading from the apex of the roof and worked his way down a chimney. He was a very tall man, his skin shaggy like a mammoth's. He must have been seven feet tall or even taller. Inexplicably, he was dressed as a woman. He was wearing a headscarf and a dark mask, as if he had just returned from a society ball.

I heard the bolt of the rifle sliding, followed by an empty click. The mountain man was already halfway down the cavern wall. He bellowed upwards at the hole in the roof. He seemed to be happy, even though he was holding his shoulder as if it was injured.

Suddenly I realised he wasn't alone. The figure of a woman, her head covered by a red headscarf, was standing by the wall. If we had been living in a fairy tale, it could have been the mountain man's grandmother. He had obviously created her – perhaps he intended her to represent his mother?

It seemed to me that what I saw before me were two birds from the same nest: the mother bird and the young adult male who refused to fly away and seek freedom: or a dragon and her mature offspring.

Magnus dropped down into the cave and lay down on the floor. I braced myself, ready for him to get up and discover me, but he remained lying there, breathing heavily. I held myself back in the shadows, peering at him through my fingers.

High above me I could hear many new voices, speaking softly in Norwegian. These whispered exchanges told me that the attacking party was now much larger; it was getting ready to enter the cave.

My stomach turned over. I was aching from fear, cold and hunger. The acid in my mouth tasted like a bitter apple. I would have been happy to shake an entire tree free of apples just to catch one, holding it safe as it fell through the leaves and branches. But more than anything, I knew that I had to get away. Hunger faded as the fight or flight instinct took over. I had to remember I was on the run, and there were some who would regard it as suspicious that I had chosen to enter the monster's cave.

In any problem there is always a solution. I started to solve this one by imagining myself already in the boat, rowing away from the island, carrying Magnus' food and water away with me. I would have escaped unseen and unknown; the inhabitants of the island would not have known who I was, or even that I had ever been on their island. In order to achieve this, I would have to be silent and invisible: a ghost. As I was already acting out my plan, the monster and the monster's mother did not see me approach them. I was able to move without alerting them to my presence because I used as cover the spate of calls taking place above my head.

I unhooked the old woman's costume from the wooden

framework and put on her garments. I turned myself into a hunchback to reduce my height. The mother was guarding the family's supplies with her life; these supplies were in a large leather sack at the end of the cave, beyond the place where her boy was struggling to find the strength to get up. I would have to separate the family from the sack; otherwise, they were not my affair. I wasn't about to kill anyone; that's not my style. I had surprise on my side. Also, I wasn't averse to dressing up.

Finally, I dismantled the wooden framework and stood in the mother figure's place. The mountain man hoisted himself into a sitting position. I remained still, confident in my plan, as he got to his feet. He was holding his right shoulder and was obviously in a lot of pain. Blood was dripping from his arm and elbow. He hauled himself to the entrance of the cave, looked up at the summit and drew his head back in again quickly. No shots were fired, no shouts were called for him to give himself up. The good guys up top didn't know how to get into the cave. They had probably thought about abseiling in but decided it would be too dangerous.

The distant whining of the helicopter as it lifted off from the jetty reached our ears. That machine would take mere moments to fly across the island and up the mountain.

Magnus picked up a rock, stepped backwards out of the cave, teetered on the cliff edge, and threw the rock at his tormentors. A young man laughed, then the older man told him off. Magnus picked up another rock and tried again. He positioned himself nearer the edge of the cliff to take a better shot. I shuffled forward, a most unlikely understudy for a monster's mother, and picked up rocks from the cave floor. When I stood next to him, I noticed a powerful stench: he smelt of goats and silage.

I handed him a rock for each hand.

He took the rocks, drew back his left arm, and then whirled around to look down at me. He said something incomprehensible and before I could answer he slipped on the ledge. He tried to regain his balance, his arms flailing about. He was going to go over, wasn't he? But if he didn't, I knew I would certainly be killed or injured. I looked at his blacked-out face, his sickly yellow eyes and they seemed to resemble the reflection I saw in my mirror. He scrambled for a handhold on the cliff, nearly made it back to solid land and then fell away into space. There was a thump and a splash as he plunged into the sea.

I tipped up the sack and discovered it was empty. The thump-thump of the helicopter was getting closer, its search-lights brightening the sea as it rounded the island. Suddenly I spotted another path, a narrow one, that led down to the sea. Using this path, I slipped and scraped my way down the cliff side, sometimes falling, sometimes coming to an abrupt halt, until I landed on a flat rock with the sea lapping over my feet.

The rowboat was approaching!

CHAPTER 27

T HEY HAD CLIMBED up Trollveggen in the dark.
Jonas was lying on his belly at the summit when the
helicopter began to hover above them. He screwed shut his
eyes, trying to protect them from the glare of its lights. 'Per,
where are you? I can't see properly. The helicopter has blinded
me. Can you see Magnus?'

Per came to lie next to him on the ground. The helicopter's
blades were snatching stones up into the air. 'Close your eyes
for a minute. Wait for your night vision to return.'

Jonas turned on to his front to shield his eyes. 'I'm not
cut out for this. You're good at it - you should join the army.'

'Maybe I will.' Per was working the action on the rifle.
'Damn, I'm out of ammunition.'

Jonas put a hand on Per's arm. 'Calm down, Per. The
commandoes are here. Don't let them hear you say anything
like that.'

'He tried to kill us.'

'I know. We acted in self-defence. You shot at him to scare
him away. You saved us all. But he's gone now, so that changes
everything. You did not act out of revenge or anger.'

Per looked over the cliff. 'Either Magnus has fallen into
the sea or he is on the rocks. I saw him slip.'

'Did you really?'

'I think so. I think he fell. He lost his footing by standing
too close to the edge. He was going to lob another rock at us.'

'It's a very weird feeling when someone tries to kill you. I still can't believe he burnt down the cabin!' The helicopter backed away, shining its lights on the sea. They both stood up and stared at the cabin, which was smoking like an oil refinery. 'Professor Nordveit is going to be so unhappy.'

'I hope Mette and Linnéa are OK.' Per scanned the sea. 'They could have ended up anywhere.'

'At least they got away. The police will find them.'

Per peered down the chimney into the cave. 'Hey, monster! Are you down there?' His voice echoed around the cavern. 'He had a fire going.'

'How did he get down into the cave?'

'Climbed down. Back against the wall, foot on the other side. There's no-one in there now. I'd like to go and have a look.' Per lay down the rifle. He started to climb into the chimney.

Erik appeared, followed by two police commandoes. 'Per, please come back here. We must go with the police and remain in their custody. You need to surrender the rifle.'

Per came back up out of the chimney. As he stood up a police commando aimed a pistol at his chest. Another officer picked up the rifle, checked the chamber was empty and slid out the bolt. 'I am not the problem,' said Per. 'The man you want is in the sea now, possibly dead, or possibly swimming away. He is a big, powerful man. I would not put anything beyond his strength.'

'There are also two young women, students, out on our motor boat, adrift with no power.' Jonas was shaking.

The commando lowered his pistol. 'We have a boat already here and there are others coming. What can you tell me about this Magnus?'

Per laughed. 'He's a student, like us, but he's a nutcase, a real live madman. The Professor tried to help him fit in, but there's no working with someone like that. He's a freak, a monster. He just hates people.'

'What's his name?' asked the officer.

Erik gave Jonas his coat. 'Per, please sit here with Jonas, you have had a terrible time.' Erik turned to the officer. 'His name is Magnus Foss. It is true he is a misfit. He gets easily frustrated with people, and doesn't fit in well, although we tried to make him feel welcome on this trip.'

'Physical description,' said the officer.

'Very tall, seven feet. Norsk, but a yellow colour to his skin, possibly as a result of a health issue. He has long stand-ing gastrointestinal problems, a form of IBS, maybe ulcers; these do not help his mood. He has been diagnosed with both depression and a personality disorder.'

'Figures,' said Per.

Jonas piped up. 'Professor. The Korean woman?'

'Another student, a young Korean woman was found dead with her brother last year. I don't know the details, but the woman was friendly with Magnus and her brother didn't like it. Their bodies were found drowned in a river. The police investigated and concluded it was an accident. Such stories did not help Magnus fit in with his peers. Yes, he was a difficult young man, but we tried to rehabilitate him.' Erik wrung his hands and looked down the hillside at the twin columns of smoke rising from the cabin, the bonfire and the toppled weather tower. 'And now he has destroyed my island.'

The two police commandoes took Jonas away a few metres for questions, and then Per. When satisfied, they led the three survivors down Trollveggen. All of them watched the death-throes of the cabin as it collapsed into the ground. Erik leant against a boulder; his whole being filled with despair. 'This has destroyed the work of four generations.'

'It can be rebuilt, Professor, bigger and better than before. You can build a new cabin, put in some hot showers, maybe a sauna.' Jonas looked his Professor steadily in the eye. 'Erect another weather tower.'

Erik could not be consoled. 'I should never have allowed Magnus to come on this trip. He trampled on the survey area and dug up the quadrats, just like a naughty child who wasn't getting his own way.'

'You did your best, Professor, but for the want of a better way of putting it, some people simply are just evil.'

They carried on their descent. Per whispered to Jonas: 'I told the police that I fired shots to warn Magnus away. I did not aim to hit him. To be honest, I could not see him well enough in the dark to take aim properly.'

'Save your testimony for the courtroom,' replied Jonas. 'Don't say any more.'

One of the police officers told them they would all be evacuated by police boat to the mainland.

Linnéa and Mette appeared at the jetty, wrapped in silver insulation blankets. 'Where is he?'

'Magnus? Gone over the cliff at the top of Trollveggen.'

Mette put her hand to her mouth. 'Accident? Suicide?' she asked?

Jonas shrugged. 'He was throwing rocks at us, then he slipped and disappeared. It was too dark to be sure how it happened.' He looked at her. 'Are you OK?'

Mette hugged Linnéa. 'We got the boat out to sea, but the current was really strong.'

'Magnus tried to stop us, but we kept him away. I even hit him with an axe I found on the boat. He snatched it and threw it back at me quickly enough.'

Mette shuddered. 'We got picked up by a tourist boat. They didn't believe our story until the captain saw the cabin burning down. Then the police arrived.'

Linnéa pointed. 'Look, there it is. The boat that found us.' In the distance a tourist boat, well lit and with its music blaring, was riding at anchor. Linnéa frowned. 'They said they'd had a strange night as well. There was a guy on board dressed like a wolf. And they lost a rowing boat, even though the sea was calm at the time.'

'What a project week!' said Jonas. 'I'll never forget it.' They watched the flames flare up from the cabin. 'This has probably ruined any chance of writing that paper you dreamed of, Professor.'

'It's ruined a lot of things - data, samples - but at least we are all safe. Except for Magnus, I suppose.'

'Are the police looking for him?'

Erik nodded. 'They need to bring in a special craft so that frogmen can search the rocks. They will do it in the morning, when it is lighter.'

'He could have escaped by then,' said Per, 'or have drowned.'

'Magnus will not get very far. There is blood on the cave floor. You must have hit him, Per, whether fatally or not.'

Mette was startled. 'You hit Magnus - what with?'

Per grinned. 'Dr Jensson had the foresight to leave a rifle in the metal locker.'

Linnéa was delighted. 'Yes! Dr Jensson is my tutor. If there is one thing we agreed about it was the need to protect ourselves against predatory males. Dr Nyland was always making excuses to her of the way he behaved.'

'Indeed, I banned Dr Nyland from taking part in these research trips.'

Per suddenly sat down on a rock and began to shake. He looked wretched. Erik asked Jonas to sit with him and warned him that Per could be in shock. Mette wrapped her silver blanket around Per and hugged him close.

After a while, a police officer strode up to them. 'It's time to go. Come with us, please.' The commandoes walked them down to the jetty and helped them into a police boat.

Erik sighed. 'This is madness. To be attacked on this island. It's university property!'

'These are bad days for the country,' said the officer. He looked at the smoking cabin. 'Is there anyone else on the island that we should know about?'

Erik shook his head and followed the officer. The police boat moved out into the sea and headed for the mainland.

CHAPTER 28

I HAD BEEN lucky, very lucky.

I didn't have the energy to pull on the oar once I'd taken control of the rowboat, so I lay down at the bottom and looked up at the light sky. I was drifting away from the island; the current was fast. I was now on its far side, the area behind the mountain. The cavern I'd penetrated had been deep inside an enormous depression in the mountain. The tiny fire the monster had built was still burning. Seabirds flew in and out of the cliffs. The helicopter had gone and there were no other boats around.

I saw I was heading into choppy waters. The waves were getting higher and breaking over the sides of the boat. I began to feel hysterical. The sea cannot be wrestled with or shot at; it is the most primordial and frightening of all the natural forces. I was getting pummelled and tossed about in the boat; my fate hung in the balance. I clung to the gunnels and kept looking up at the sky. As the waves crashed over me, I could only shiver, knowing that I just had to wait it out and hope for the best.

I thought of my parents, of Melanie, and asked myself how I came to be clinging on to a boat in a storm in the Norwegian Sea.

Give up, Bjarne had said, but what he really meant was to trust in a higher power. This seemed exactly the right time to put the idea to the test. I was soaked to the skin, cold, hungry and not a little scared. I kept my eyes on the sky, blotting out other thoughts by noticing how pretty it was. Birds were crying overhead. My eyes were stinging from the salt water. I took the wolf skin out of the satchel and held it to my chest as if it were a comforter.

Giving up would be easy. My hearing grew more muffled, my vision dulled. A warmth crept over my body, but I knew I was losing heat fast. Hypothermia was setting in. I gave up my shield and spear and my brothers bowed their heads around me. I detached myself from the scene; looking down on the young man in the boat as his arms and legs thrashed about.

Perhaps it was the flotsam-like quality of my craft that saved me. The boat skipped off the surface of the waves rather than pitching beneath them. I didn't try any heroics. When the sea had become calmer I hung my head over the side and vomited out a stomach's worth of sea water. My body was aching all over, as if I had been pushed through Bjarne's mangle. I heard the birds crying again and thought what a beautiful sound it was.

When the tale of this story is told, or when its song is sung, the bard will probably declaim that the hero was a local, a Norwegian freedom fighter. He was a brave young man who lost his life by storming the cave and sending the monster and - alas - himself on a last flight over the mountainside. No one would know about the thief who stealthily crept up the hill and, once the monster had been killed, as unobtrusively crept away again.

I was picked up by a vessel whose crew were some of the toughest men I'd ever seen. Beards, long hair, yellow boots, thick sweaters, the lot: merchant seamen who hadn't seen land for a month.

They hauled me out of the boat, using a net, and dumped me on a freezing metal bench at the back of their ship. Again, I hung over the side to throw up, retching and coughing, until nothing was left inside me but small gasps of air. The gulls looked on, curious. One of the fishermen – he may have been the captain because everyone seemed to defer to him - came by at frequent intervals to keep an eye on me. The man pulled at my shirt and then pulled at his own. I didn't know what he meant and in any case I couldn't move. He then hauled me to my feet, placing his hands under my arms, and in one violent move wrenched off my shirt. The action exposed my many sores, cuts, boils, and blisters. The captain poured clean water over my skin and applied a thick ointment to the wounds. He barked some orders in Russian.

I spent most of my time on all fours on the deck, as the ship was tossed up and down in the swell. A day or two passed, during which I developed a fever. I was given water to drink, which I could keep down only for a short time before my stomach hurled it out again. Someone gave me two white tablets and more water. Eventually I began to feel better. I ate a small amount of bread and this time managed to keep down both food and water.

The sailors strode around the ship, unperturbed by the rough seas. I saw ice in the sea; we passed a glacier. My legs were still like jelly, so I was obliged to crawl everywhere. At night I slept in a small room, wrapped up in blankets and a tarpaulin. The crew didn't want me to see what they got up to on the rest of the ship, but to be honest I wasn't interested. My room was draughty and grew astonishingly cold at night: not the kind of cold that numbs hands and makes it awkward to fit keys into locks, but the kind that prevents shivering and causes fast, shallow breathing and a blue tinge around the lips. One night I was so ill that the captain blindfolded me and led me into a more sheltered place in the ship.

Slowly my head cleared and I was able to regain my concentration. The captain spoke more to me when he visited but I could manage no more than a sad shrug. One day I was given a foil packet containing cereal flakes mixed with honey. The sugar stung my tongue and set my teeth on edge, but after I had eaten it I was allowed out on deck. The bad weather had dissipated. The boat was now moving parallel to the coast, which offered many interesting nooks and crannies that could have been explored if we'd landed. Green cliffs plunged down into fjords. Thin waterfalls fell into the sea. Colourful wooden huts and houses appeared on the hills above the rocks.

I gave myself a talking-to. 'You chose this life, so understand that you have made your bed and must lie in it.' The boat was moving more slowly now. The captain appeared to be searching for something.

I took the wolf skin out of my satchel. It had got so wet that it was ruined, the head already beginning to decompose. The skin was moulting, the fur coming away in tufts. I threw it into the sea and watched the birds pull it apart. I stretched my arms up to the sky and smiled at the sores that were now healing on my chest.

There were beautiful cliffs to the port side, lit yellow by the sun, looking both striking and strange among the green hills. A light fog came rolling up off the sea. The captain nudged his vessel towards the shoreline, beyond which were red huts clustered on the cliffs. He simulated walking by moving two fingers of one hand on his other upturned hand. I nodded. When we arrived at the wharf, a woman with a bag on her back came down from the hills to meet the captain.

The two kissed and talked for a while as I stood and shivered. I had survived a fight with a dreadful sea monster and had finally reached this place. It was a long way north, but this was a beautiful land. I felt the odd freakish gust of warm wind, perhaps a signal that the summer was ending. I recognised a few stray words: 'villa' and 'Martin'. There was no mention of Sigrid or Tromsø.

The woman pulled a blanket out of her bag and wrapped it over my shoulders. Her eyes smiled as I thanked her. She embraced the captain again and he returned to his ship. The woman led me up the cliff path. I stood with one foot raised up on a rock and watched him leave. Soon he was eclipsed by the fog.

CHAPTER 29

THE WATER WAS cold but Magnus the Great was a strong swimmer. Once he had got his good arm going and had started to pull through the waves, he thought he had a chance of surviving, even though the sea was icy. But soon his shoulder was complaining too much and his bad arm was leaking blood from his wound. His spirit had the will to survive, but his body was very much weakened.

Magnus held his breath at the times that the sea surged over him. The slap of the waves knocked the air out of his lungs. He kicked his legs instinctively to stay afloat and pulled with his left arm only through the water. The cold was seeping towards his heart. He tried to swim on, turning his head from side to side, gasping for breath. He was able to inhale easily enough, but the oxygen didn't do much to revive his muscles.

His chest was burning hot now; the pain from his shoulder was spreading down his right arm. The trust fund girl had hit him with a hatchet! He admired someone with a bit of spark, but it had hurt, maybe more than he had realised at the time. The blade must have pierced his coir coat. He wished he had known there was a hatchet in the boat; he could have used it earlier. Never mind; next time, next island. There were many islands off the coast; not all of them would be inhabited. He just had to reach one of them and drag himself to the shore.

He paused for a moment and trod water, kicking out his legs as he floated upright. The sea sparkled around him and invited him to push himself under and end it all quickly. His left leg stopped moving, paralysed by the cold. He kicked again with his right leg and tried to swim on.

A boat was approaching. Who could possibly have come out to save him in such a high sea? He was impressed. What type of boat was it? He could only see the prow of the boat approaching; he couldn't make out the rest. He blinked away the salt and focused on the mainland, where the moon was hanging high above the snow-sprinkled mountains. In the gloaming dark shapes grew legs and became night animals. The sea brought the sun's rays across the rippling waves, reaching Svindel on a trajectory of solar stepping stones. A shoal of fish swam past him, breaking the water in dashes of lights, and then they were gone.

Svindel was a beautiful sight, lit up as it was by the burning cabin and the bonfire. There were many boats at the jetty now, all too late for the party. The weather tower was lying across the cabin, like a fisherman exhausted by a storm who had collapsed on his bunk. Trollveggen looked like a bruise: its red top was angry, like the rubor of inflamed tissue. The Professor and the students had found a rifle and they had shot at him, he reflected. It should have been the other way round.

The boat came nearer. It was much too small to be a lifeboat, unless it was a class D, a rubber boat that could be ridden up on the rocks to search for survivors. No need to search any longer, captain, I'm right here, taking on water, sinking lower, trying to come back up, but sinking still.

He fought the panic rising inside him. He was tired, exhausted. The fall from the cliff had winded him and wounded him very badly. He swallowed a mouthful of water. Choking and gasping, he floundered as a large wave hit him.

'Help!' he cried, as he surfaced. The birds cried back. Where was his sack? He'd forgotten the sack: it was made from an elephant bladder. Inflate it and he would have a life raft. But he'd lost the sack along with everything else.

He turned on his back and at last managed to get his breath; but his legs were sinking, pulling him under. He felt like a man whose skeleton had dissolved, his flesh turned to jelly. His limbs lay, sagging, in the water. Gradually he was losing his battle with the lapping waves. The water splashed up over his face, but he fought back, breathing in another great draught of air. By chance he suddenly bumped into a rock; he made a grab for it. Perhaps now he might survive; but the rock had cut open the flesh on his hand and he couldn't grasp its slimy surface. He looked up at the night sky and waited.

He sensed that the boat was drawing up close to him. It was a wreck: it had been badly damaged in a storm; only half of it was left. How the figure piloting the boat had managed to row a half-boat across the sea, he could not tell. The boat was covered with seaweed, as if it had just risen up from the bottom of the sea. The figure put down the oars and stood up. He was a tall man. He wore a hooded coat. The birds were screaming above him. The man in the rowing boat was screaming Magnus's name. Seaweed dripped from the man's head and shoulders as he leaned over to speak to him.

Look, there is an island approaching. There will be friendly people there, ready to take care of you. They will offer you warmth and shelter, food and drink. Just be nice to them. You have come a long way. Never mind the rocks; even if they cut your arms and legs, you will be safe. Never mind the water that slows your breathing. Aim for the light and the ever-widening sun.

You are Magnus the Great, King of Trollveggen.
You can do this.

ACKNOWLEDGEMENTS

I AM FORTUNATE to have Linda Bennett as my editor, and I would like to thank her for tightening and polishing the manuscript. I'd also like to thank Chris and Jen Hamilton-Emery, and Emma Dowson, for their support.